CHAPTER 1

THE CITY OF NEW ORLEANS

Arlo Guthrie's song, "The City of New Orleans" keeps playing over and over in my head, "fifteen cars and fifteen restless riders, three conductors, twenty-five sacks of mail… as the President of Joe's college drones on and on about the school's pride in winning their first college bowl game. Joe, Phillip, Julie, and I have seen the damn trophy more times than a Budweiser commercial during the Super Bowl.

My mind keeps flashing back to the long train ride we took leaving New York and winding up here in southern Florida. It seemed like a great idea at the time.

A college president should not have an office the size of the football field. He has civil war swords littering the walls. If this story goes any further, I have the mind to take one off the wall and cut him in half. I'm sure my son would get thrown out of school for that. Robert Johnson, a fifty-year-old proper southern gentleman with plastic hair and a potbelly that strains his starched white shirt and college tie, paces the room like a rat on crack. It seems he has played sleuth until we've gotten down here, and he is quite pleased with himself. Phillip is busy taking notes, or so I think. I make my way over to him and peer over his shoulders. On his pad, he has written the word *idiot* about a hundred times. It's good to see he's as impressed as I am with General Lee. Julie and Joe are amusing themselves by spinning the large world globe in one corner until it spins off its axis and rolls around the corner of the office. They scramble to put it back in its wood frame.

It's time to end this, but Johnson will not stop. ... "Now these are just rumors like I said before."

Way before I say to myself, I can't believe he's going to re-tell us his theory about the two thieves leaving on a train for California, he starts over again. Please no.

"I'll bet my last nickel they are either leaving or have left by train I remind you that is only a hunch but then again I did have the hunch about us winning the big game."

"Uncle," I scream. Nobody gets it but Phillip who heads for the door. I grab the piece of paper from Johnson's hand. He has written down the supposed thief's address and number. If we do not take our leave right now, they will not need a train to get away, they could crawl away, and we still would not catch them. Being as rude as we are by just walking out does not even faze Mr. Johnson. I hold the door for Julie and Joe and wave goodbye, shaking hands would take too long.

We arrived at the train station two hours ago, went straight to a local hotel which is close to the campus and drove our rental car to the president's office, and then got a quick tour of Joe's college dorm. The Spanish architecture throughout the lush grounds gives me the feeling I'm in a five-star resort. The college girls give it the feel of the Playboy mansion. Joe leads us through the maze of buildings to the dorm area. The dorms are set aside from the stately brick and column classrooms and after seeing Joe's room I can understand why.

Julie has experienced this before since she is the only one among us that has gone to college. It's a wonder the kids can get anything done while living like this. MTV has shown this life on TV and parents still send their kids away to school. I think deep down inside the fathers really can't wait to visit their kids hoping for a glimpse of the girls they have seen on MTV.

Joe's dorm room reminds me of the motel we had in Key West, but smaller. Two single beds on one side and two desks face to face at the window. The two chests of drawers almost covering up the tiny closets don't leave room for the five of us to stand without touching feet. While the uncomfortable silence hangs in the stale air, I think it is a good time to get some sun and think about how we got here and where we need to go. New York City this is not. Finding a place for a quick drink or cup of coffee to think will be impossible though staring at 20-year-old girls will be a better distraction. The problem is they all look alike. Three overly cheery girls pass by and wave, "Hey Mr. Biltmore." I guess Joe introduced us earlier on our tour, it's hard to remember all these polite kids.

In the last twenty minutes, I have met four thousand kids and they all are disgustingly nice. I find a quiet tree to lean against and think. I hate when cases smell from the beginning. This Johnson character was OK, but his story of the missing college football bowl money from the bookkeeper's safe sounds too easy. I hate to admit it, but I know nothing about how these big-time football programs on college campuses work. I do know that just by walking around campus I can readily see that sports drive this bus. Before coming down here I did some quick research and was able to dig up information on the football program. The coach makes a freakin fortune. $ 3.6 million a year!! I can't seem to get that out of my head when Julie and Phillip walk out of the dorm and over to my shady spot.

"Where do we go from here?" Julie finishes her question as she reaches me.

"I'm trying to figure this out. It's an inside job."

Phillip doesn't let me finish. "Let's think about this. This is a business transaction in the millions, right? Do we think they received payment in the form of a check?"

Julie and I look at each other.

"Come on guys, something this big, from a huge reputable organization, they would wire the money into a safe and secure school account," Phillip states.

"He's got a point." Julie insists.

"Then why are we here? I think we need to go back to Johnson's office and ask some more questions. Let's leave Joe out of this until we find out something we can sink our teeth into."

As I finish, we start for the president's office.

"Any idea where…."

Phillips points in the direction of the administration building in the distance and on the hill. I know we were just there but everything looks the same…I pull out my cell phone and inform Joe that we are returning to Johnson's office to ask some more questions.

"OK, I understand." I shut the phone.

"Joe says to tread softly. Johnson may act cordial but the only person with more power in this part of the state is the football coach and that includes the governor who was born ten minutes from here."

CHAPTER 2

PUNT

As we enter the inner office of President Johnson, his secretary, the doty Miss Lee, fifty-eight going on one hundred, and an almost direct descendent of Robert E Lee, is gingerly knocking on the huge pair of walnut carved doors. There is no way anyone can hear that soft tap on the other side.

"What seems to be the problem, Miss Lee?" I inquire.

With a terrified look on her face, she mumbles, "I heard a loud phone conversation, a glass shatter, and a muffled thud."

Phillip and I try the door but there is no way we are going to budge this slab of wood. I look at Miss Lee, "Key?"

Miss Lee runs to her purse and produces a key from her key chain. I make a mental note of that. She pushes the key in, and Phillip turns the doorknob. I step in front of Miss Lee and Julie holds her by the shoulders, we are all expecting the worse. President Johnson is slumped over in his chair and his water glass is knocked over. An overpowering smell of gas almost makes me throw up. I see on the opposite wall of the window a red laser scope light aiming at the trophy case. Julie and I have the same reaction, we grab Miss Lee and Phillip and run from the door slamming the large wooden doors behind us and throwing ourselves onto the ground. The explosion rattles the entire building. Thank goodness the building was built 85 years ago. The masonry construction and two-inch thick doors kept the four of us alive. I am not so sure about Johnson. I grab for the door.

"I would not do that," shouts Phillip.

Phillip gets up, reaches for his handkerchief, and uses that to insulate his hands against the brass doorknob and the scorching heat.

Julie urges Miss Lee to get help while the three of us stand in the doorway surveying what used to be a pretty nice room. I look at Johnson and the first thing that comes to mind is – closed casket.

All three of us realize that we do not have a lot of time. We split up instantly and look for any clues as to what caused this gas explosion. Gas explosion? I do not see any gas heating radiators. An old building like this would have the old steam radiators as I had in the bar. Julie is kneeling next to the charred fireplace. I watch her pick up something off the floor and put it in her pocket. Phillip is at the trophy case with a bent head and a puzzled look on his face.

I hear sirens approaching.

"Let's go."

The three of us hurry out.

Chapter 3

Re-Cap

I was still living in NYC as Joe went off to school to Southern Florida College of the Extreme Sunshine to study writing, (I'm not sure what that means or how you study writing, I thought you just did it.) We thought it would be a good compromise. He goes to school in Florida, and I would try retiring there someday. Yes, I won the bet between us. The last case was appealing for him to choose between being a full-time private eye, but I understand doing what one wants is particularly important and agreed to let him go to college while I transplant myself to a place where I can work, fish, and enjoy the weather throughout the year. It happened a bit sooner than I expected. When Joe called with this case I moved fast to move down here. So, I gave up the glamour of bar life and applied for a private investigation license here in Florida.

I took Joe all over the world in search of the perfect fishing spots. In those years, he has learned about the world and became a well-rounded kid. All this time together has left a great mark on him as well as me, including the time in Spain when we got involved in a missing

Contessa case and we were almost tried for treason. He was twelve and thought it was extremely exciting. He wrote about his summer in a Spanish jail when he went back to school in September. I had to explain to his teachers that he was never in any danger. (Including some social workers who had no sense of humor.)

Phillip Meli had no family to speak of and always loved the thought of getting out of New York City. He could write anywhere. Money is no issue for him.

Tom Caruso has decided to take a little place to rent in Key Largo with his wife. After a long heart-to-heart talk, he decided to retire from the police department but wanted to hold onto his NYC roots. Just not in the winter.

Acting on a whim was never part of my personality. When I threw the keys of the bar to Bobby that fateful day, I had the pounding in the back of my head that I did something wrong. New is always tough, but I never knew how tough until we started the day-to-day grind of getting a business off the ground in Florida. Now it is not like opening a store, hiring employees, getting banks in line, merchandise ordered, and all that crap. I wanted to be a legit investigator. Phillip and I found a little town near Key Largo to settle into. We could easily get on the interstate, rent is cheap, dock space was close by, (out the back door and down three steps) and best of all Caruso's old chief inspector of the New York City Detectives was the so-called mayor of the hamlet. Getting my gun license transferred down here took two trips to Starbucks and a signature.

The easy part of the move was that Julie asked for and received, (with a lot of help from a certain admiral) a transfer to the FBI office in Miami. We are still trying to figure out what path our relationship is going. The nice part is that she will help with this case while on leave.

Julie, Philip, and I needed a few weeks back in New York to handle some final closeouts of our northern lives. Joe came back to New York to grab some last-minute things and help me close up the apartment over a short weekend. Joe headed back down to Florida to start the school year. In my infinite wisdom, I thought a train trip would be fun. By the time we hit Newark New Jersey I owed both Philip and Julie a big dinner once we arrived in Florida. Philip tried to get off the train in Baltimore and fly the rest of the way, but the area scared him.

CHAPTER 4

IMPLAUSIBLE

The timing could not have been more perfect. A medic is tending to Miss Lee on the limestone steps of the administration building. She is babbling on about a bomb and dear old Mr. Johnson looking like a charred hot dog. I guess it's the best she can come up with considering what she has just witnessed. She points to us as we make our way out of the commotion. The young female medic does not pay attention to Miss Lee's frantic pointing at us as we hurriedly walk by.

The streets around the administration building are filling up with town police cars, campus police cars, fire engines, and medical trucks. I figured we will get dragged back into this sooner or later once Miss Lee is coherent enough to tell the police about us but I want to get our stories straight and find out what my colleagues think. Phillip and Julie just keep their heads bowed like me and follow close by. We make our way to the center of the quad where hundreds of students have materialized. My cell phone is going off in my pocket.

"I had nothing to do with it. We tried to get into the office right before the big bang. We are in the middle of the quad, right by the statue of someone. Meet us there."

"Joe," I say to Phillip and Julie.

"What did you pick up from the floor?" I ask Julie.

Julie pulls from the pocket of her jeans a piece of gray clay. I take it, squeeze it then smell it. I am clueless. I hand it to Phillip.

"You were staring at the trophy case with a strange look on your face. We know that someone shot at the trophy case. We all saw the laser light. We all smelled gas too."

Phillip is about to start his hypothesis when Joe comes running up. Phillip waits for him.

"We all saw the laser light from the rifle. I also noticed the valve to the gas fireplace open," Starts Phillip.

"Wouldn't Mr. Johnson have noticed someone opening up the valve to let gas into the room?" Julie asks.

"The valve only opens the gas line; you still need to hit the remote for the fireplace to ignite the flame. Our killer used that clay you found to make a little cup over the gas pipe and put some liquid that would eventually eat through the clay then through the pipe causing the gas to leak into the room. When he was in the room he also hid something within the trophy case that would give enough charge so when he shot the trophy case with the hidden charge it caused a little explosion mixed with the gas-filled room and ka blowie."

The three of us look on in amazement and disbelief. It seemed like we were staring at Phillip for an hour before anyone of us could say something. I think it hit us all at the same time.

"OK, makes sense," All three of us in unison say.

Julie decides to go the law enforcement route, "Let's say this is what happened; one, if we tell this story to the police, they will hold us for questioning for hours; two if it is true, we are looking at real professional hired killers and not just some simple grand larceny case and a missing person."

"Dad."

Ignoring Joe, I chime in," We have no client right now."

"DAD!" Joe loudly.

We all look at Joe who is pointing towards the administration building and all see about ten policemen with guns drawn running towards us with Miss Lee pointing the way.

Thinking quickly, "They will split us up to question us. NO THEORIES!"

The policeman in charge gets to us fast, we put our hands up. The other policemen are steps behind.

"Put your hands down quickly. Come with us, you could be in danger."

We all do a double-take, shrug, and follow quickly behind the head cop while the others surround us.

I like these guys. Back in NYC Caruso would never have done this – he always blamed me first.

CHAPTER 5

ACT DUMB

We have now attracted more attention with our little escorts than if they would have done this discreetly, but what the hell. Julie is chuckling at the show of force. We are led back to the administration building and into a ground-floor office to the right of the massive entrance doors. As we enter the empty office, all but one of the officers leaves us. The lone officer leans against the double doors protecting either us or someone outside the office. I am not sure which.

There is a large wooden five-foot-high counter facing the doors and a large workspace behind the counter. Two large offices are flanking either side of the open workspace. The workspace furniture is very sleek, and the computer screens are very new.

"Well dad, what do you think? They shut down the entire campus when the blast occurred and broadcast over our cell phones not to leave our dorm rooms and classrooms. I was already out of my room when it happened. Do you think it was an accident of some sort?"

Phillip is snooping around the office and Julie is leaning against the counter with arms folded. I am pacing and trying to think.

"This was ....."

Just as I start, a burly man in a cheap lightweight suit comes in and overwhelms the room.

"You were saying, Mr. Biltmore?" The bulk hits me with his laser eyes and a hard stare.

I figured I would start with a question of my own and deflect what the hell he was doing. "And you are...?"

"Federal Marshal Copeland."

That unfolds Julie's arms and straightens her up. Phillip stops snooping around long enough to at least pay attention. A regular cop would have bored the hell out of him.

"OK I will bite, why is a federal marshal here, and how so quickly?"

"It does not work that way. I ask the questions and if it goes well I will let you go back outside and you can continue your business. Oh, I want to warn you, that little 'hit' was meant for you as well."

OK, now he has our interest. I am trying not to even twitch a muscle to give away my panic. Phillip on instinct walks away from the windows and leans against the cement block and wood-paneled walls to my right. I notice Julie fishing through the pocket of her jeans, looking for her FBI credentials I figure. I slowly clutch her forearm to stop her.

"We know you are FBI Miss Waters. Look guys, you all have very impressive friends in different positions, and believe it or not, I am here to help you and my case."

This room is very cold since there are only six in here and the air conditioning is on for thirty workers and kids coming and going all day. This Copeland character is beading up around the collar. Either he has malaria or his pressure is building. He removes his jacket and I see his service weapon, an automatic with 15 rounds at the ready. I glance down at his ankle and sure enough, I see the bulge. Copeland catches my eye but does not react.

"Let's stop dancing." Copeland walks past the counter and into the office to the right. We follow. He stops and looks around the room and spots an under-counter refrigerator. He opens it and produces a water bottle and leaves the door open.

"Help yourselves and sit down."

Of course we do. Copeland heads around the large mahogany desk and helps himself to a chair and sits down. This is a bit of a powerplay. Him sitting behind the desk and us sitting in front of him. There are two leather and wood low slung chairs in front of the desk. I gently put my hand on Julie's back for her to grab one chair as I take the other. Joe and Phillip can stand.

Copeland opens the water bottle and takes a long slug, dribbling some and wiping his mouth with his cheap sleeve. I'm surprised the water did not bead up.

"OK, let's start. We know it was a hit. We have been following a dwarf albino from Canada for three months. He escaped from prison there five months ago. He found his way to Cuba through Canada about a month ago. Go ahead ask – why would the US Federal Marshals care about an escaped con from Canada. Let me tell you why." Copeland leans back in the swivel chair and catches himself from falling over backward. I smirk inside. He's too big and sweaty to smirk to his face – yet.

"Dwarf albino?" asks an incredulous Phillip.

"Small white-haired guy, is that better? Jeez, I thought you New Yorkers would enjoy a little sarcasm."

Copeland looks around the room at three deadpan faces. Joe looks puzzled.

"As you may or may not know college football is big-time money to these schools. Any school that can consistently get to a bowl game means money and ego, especially to the school trustees and the boosters. We're talking bribes, rule violations, kids never seeing the inside of a classroom, and more bribes. The people doing the bribing are taking bribes themselves. This year alone we tracked one school's entire athletic department on a cruise to the islands paid for by the NCAA bowl rule committee."

Nothing I cannot see on ESPN. Where is he going?

"What does this have to do with us?" Julie blurts out ahead of me.

"We know you have been brought into this mess to find a missing booster and a professor who our dear departed Mr. Johnson thinks stole his bowl funds."

"Wouldn't these funds be electronically transferred into bank accounts and not sitting around like money from a cash register?" Phillips surmises.

"Of course, they would and they were," Offers up Copeland.

I sense there is more.

"We are talking about missing cash, bribe money. We think that Johnson was head of the so-called slush fund for the NCAA, all major sports networks, and every booster group for the major bowls. We have a feeling he kept all that from you."

I must ask, "How much do we think is missing?" I hold my breath on this one.

"We're not sure, only rumors and with the amount of panic that has besieged these groups, we think it could be over ten million in cash." Copeland freely offers up.

"Who killed Mr. Johnson?" Joe asks which makes us all turn our heads.

"His partners, I figure. One less person who knows where the money is the better the plan. But why get us too?" Phillip throws out to Copeland knowing it's a silly question.

"Mr. Biltmore has a quite the reputation with many different types of people; the underworld, government, and law enforcement. We got wind of you coming down here. A certain police captain and an FBI boss asked us as a professional courtesy to keep an eye on you. Our hunch was right."

My head was hurting, "Where do we go from here?"

"We'd like you to keep an open mind. We think the killer or killers are on their way out of the state by now. They probably think you're dead or in protective custody. We think you will be contacted by someone to stay on the case. We'd like you to also."

"I'm sure you would. Not sure how my friends here like to be clay pigeons for a bunch of hired killers working for the NCAA."

"We never said they work for…"

Interrupting Copeland was the least I could do, "New York sarcastic talking. Let's us think about it, where can we be in touch?"

Julie and I get up and walk to the door. Phillip is already walking out and Joe is right behind him. Copeland gets up and meets us at the door and produces a card.

"Stay in touch. I know you can take care of yourself. But I think these people have a lot to lose."

"If they didn't, I would not be here. Speak soon."

I follow my team out the office door and back into the hallway and out into the sunshine. The police forensic team has the whole building blocked off. The bomb squad is picking through the debris outside the building around the window. We all stop watching the action. I think we all have the same thought.

"Do we offer our help?" Julie ponders.

Before I get to answer, Phillip chimes in, "We just have a theory for now. No need to throw a monkey wrench into the situation with a bunch of conjecture."

"My thoughts exactly," I lead the way away from the building. "We need a place to think of our next move away from here. I guess we can go to our hotel."

"Not sure that's a good idea Dad, if someone is watching and waiting for you they'll have the hotel staked out. There is a nice quiet bar on the water about thirty minutes from here."

Phillip puts his arm around Joe, "Your dad never would have thought of that. I'm glad you're here Joe."

"Should I check in with the office and find out if this Copeland character is on the level?" Julie offers.

"Not a bad idea, though I would be careful who you check with," I offer up.

CHAPTER 6

LOOSE WIRE

We reach the car. Everyone walks around the car to a door.

I scream "Away from the car."

We have been working together for a while now and these alert drives everyone to do a quick about-face and walk away from the car. I back away slowly. I need to make sure there is no one else standing by their car as we move away from our rental and a safe distance away.

"What did you see dad?"

"Wires on the ground by the front tire. Looked like detonating wires, can't be sure though. It looks wrong."

"What do we do, we need to keep people away from the car but we cannot just stare at it." Julie states.

"No one is watching, or they would have set it off when we were next to the car. It must be rigged for either a door slam or when the car starts." Phillip figures.

I am not sure what to do. I notice three kids walking towards the lot and right behind the ticking time bomb. I figure as long as they keep walking they are safe. Julie starts for them and I grab her arm.

"If you call to them and stop them behind the car, you never know what will happen."

We watch in silence as the three kids get into an old 1978 Chevy Impala. As luck would have it they pull out of their parking space directly behind us. Please don't hit our car. They drive nice and carefully from reverse to drive to reverse to drive from reverse to drive – small spots, big car. I love careful drivers. They are finally out of their spot and start pulling away from the danger zone. Twenty feet from the parking space the Chevy backfires blowing up our rental car.

"Did you take the extra insurance?" Phillip mocks.

"I think it is better if we just walk away." I declare.

I notice the kids are out of their car and seem ok, a bit shaken but ok. I don't want to stick around for more lectures and questions today. We all split up and walk slowly away from the small still burning inferno.

"Where do we go now, dad?"

"Let's walk where it's crowded. I'm hoping the killer will have a conscience and not try and take us out in public."

Julie laughs, "I guess the blowing up of an office building and rigging your car to explode is a private matter."

"I was trying to make Joe feel better."

"It did not work. There is a small coffee shop right off-campus. We won't need the car at least." Joe does not wait for an answer, he heads between two buildings, down an asphalt patch through a small parking lot. As we come to the wide-open lot Joe continues to walk straight ahead. Julie, Phillip, and I do a complete stop and survey of the parking lot not knowing what to look for. We shrug and pick up the pace as we hurry through the half-empty lot.

Joe is first to the coffee shop, scanning the booths as we enter. The place is pretty empty except for the rear booth. Four kids are stuffed into the small booth drinking coffee and laughing. We sit in a booth; Joe grabs a chair to stick on the end of the booth to keep us from crushing each other. We wait in silence as the waitress/college kid makes her way over.

"Do you have scotch?" Phillip asks, half kidding.

"What type of coffee can I get you?" Offers up the perky kid, oblivious to Phillip's question.

"Espresso, regular, regular, decaf," we all chime in over each other.

"Now what dad, we don't have a client anymore. I guess this case is dead."

"Burnt is more like it. I'd like to drum up something out of this mess. There seems to be a lot of money missing and I am sure someone would pay very nicely for us to retrieve it."

Julie looks puzzled, "How do you expect to get hired when we have no idea who is on what side."

The girl brings our coffee which stops the conversation. When she turns and walks away Phillip starts his thought.

"We continue snooping around as if we got rehired by someone else to find the money. We make believe we still have a client. We can even set up phony meetings. This will bring someone out of the woods to approach us… or try and kill us again. Jamaica, when do you think Caruso will be headed down here?"

"I think he's down here already. I think he arrived ahead of his wife to open the house and to catch up with us for some fishing before the rest of the family arrives. Why?"

Phillip continues, "We might need his help. I hate to say this, but I would feel more comfortable if you had…"

Julie raises her hands in mock horror, "Please don't even suggest Jamaica needs his guns."

"I prefer someone to have a gun, even you. We have no self-defense weapons except hiding behind a couple of these college kids." Phillip concludes.

I decided to ignore the wisecracks. "By the way, I never got to ask you about your theory of how the office exploded. How did you come up with that method of blowing up the room?"

Phillip gets a shy look on his face, "The Mechanic – the movie, the first one. Charles Bronson and Jan Michael Vincent are hired killers and Bronson uses this method at the beginning of the movie."

"So, we are looking for a college football fanatic who likes old movies?" Julie laughs.

"Let's think about how we start this little scheme of ours to find a client. The first thing we'll need…" I let out.

"…is another rental car." Joe lets out which gets a small laugh from the crew.

"Very good Joe, though it is true. Anyone got a credit card we can put a car under? I say we start with some of the football boosters. In a few days, we will see who Johnson's real friends are at his wake. We will need a good camera and then someone to identify all the people in the pictures. That's task one. Julie, any way you can check into work and see if this killing is creating any buzz. Also, check on this Copeland character, see if he is someone we can trust. I would think that some law enforcement agency had to be looking into this crazy football stuff besides us. Joe, you need to stay with classes but in the meantime check with Caruso and see if he is free to come to visit you in school without alarming him of this little mess. Phillip you and I will get a new car and provisions to keep this hoax up."

Joe gets up to leave. "I have a class in an hour, I will call you later."

"OK, keep your eyes open. We are not out of the woods yet."

"Will do."

Joe walks out of the coffee shop and into the warm air. He looks around and trots across the street through the parking lot and towards the dorms. Phillip, Julie, and I watch in silence.

"Do you think…."

"I think they will only come after me if they want to silence this investigation. I don't think we are dealing with underworld criminal types who will do anything to silence us."

"You are right, these people are worse, they panic easily. This is their only scam. It's all or nothing. Not professional and can be talked into anything by anybody," Julie states.

"Not very comforting. Let's meet at the motel in an hour."

I throw a twenty on the table and head for the door and into the sunlight to what, follow Joe to class? I did that fifteen years ago when I followed the school bus three blocks to his school and hid across the street behind a garbage dumpster every day for a week while he got off the bus and into his school.

CHAPTER 7

THE SON ALSO RISES

I stay well back of Joe as he makes his way to his dorm to pick up his books than to class, I presume. The warm air feels good. Am I acting like a crazed overprotective father? Probably. I guess a building blowing up and a car explosion gives me the right. Looking around at all these innocent faces makes me think why the hell I wanted him to be part of this business. My last two cases have been a lot more violent than anything I have had over the past thirty years. I was getting bored with just following people though. Boy, all these kids look young and the girls are very pretty. I don't know how a guy studies with this type of distraction all around him all the time.

I would rather just walk around campus all day and just enjoy the scenery and the great weather. Oh shit, where did he go? I don't remember where his dorm is and there are dozens of kids milling about.

I head between two low-lying buildings, they seem to be dorms by the kids that are hanging outside sunning themselves.

Joe scares the crap out of me as he seems to jump out from behind a building.

"Dad, why are you following me?"

"No, just…"

"I will be OK, I decided I wanted to be in the family business while going to college remember? I picked up a few things over the years, like knowing when someone is tailing me. Like now."

"Phillip and Julie got me spooked. I don't know much about these guys who are trying to get us off the case. The last case up in New York was very clear. This is confusing and I wanted to make sure these bad guys did not try and get to me through you."

"OK, I'm going to class and will call you as soon as I am done."

I start walking away.

"Joe."

"Yeah, dad?"

"How do I get back to the coffee shop?"

Joe begins to laugh. Then stops, "Why don't I point you in the direction so you don't get lost."

I can see by his eyes that something is wrong. I need to play along with it. Joe puts his arm on my shoulder and guides me to the path back where I just came from. As we turn the corner, I see her. I have seen her face before but never connected it, just thought I saw this same woman twice on the same day. She is trying to look natural standing behind the building. How the hell do you look natural standing next to a building? She looks nervous in her baseball hat and large movie star sunglasses.

Joe points towards the parking lot through the trees, "Take that path there, and across the small lot is the coffee shop."

"Thanks, have a nice time in class, call Julie and tell her I am on my way back and we will head to the hotel."

When I see an opening, I break for the woman. She did not expect me to run for her. She turns and runs down the path. God, she is fast. As she turns away from my direction she runs right into Phillip and Julie. Julie slams her to the ground.

"Nice backup," I chime in.

"We figured if you were worried about Joe, we should be worried about you. Your hunches are usually surprisingly good." Retorts Phillip.

"You learned a lot sitting at the end of my bar."

Julie helps the woman to her feet while holding her arm bent behind her back.

A few kids have seen the commotion, but Joe is explaining something to them and they disperse. He walks over to us. Nice job getting that taken care of.

"Who is she dad?"

Julie, Phillip, and I turn and stare at the woman. She looks very uncomfortable as Julie twists her arm around her back.

"Please stop Mr. Biltmore. I will explain."

I reach for Julie to let go.

"Go ahead."

The woman has a scared shit look on her face. "I'm the missing professor you were hired to find."

CHAPTER 8

HIDE IN PLAIN SIGHT

"I don't like just standing here,"

"I agree Jamaica, lets at least move and find some place where it will be a little safer where someone won't take a shot at us," Julie exclaims.

"How about the library?" Joe offers.

We all look at him.

"Pretty good idea. I am sure we will be safe there. Joe, why don't you and Phillip's head over to the library and find a place where we can talk."

Phillip follows Joe back up the path towards the center of the campus.

I turn towards our professor, "I'm hoping you know where the library is?"

I watch as Phillip and Joe make their way in the center of the quad towards a limestone and glass multi-level structure, which I assume is the library.

"Jamaica, that's quite a walk ..."

"Is there any way we can get into the library from another building?" I direct to the professor.

"You mean like a tunnel?"

"That would be great, for you and us."

"No."

Julie looks at her with disgust.

As it happens only in these situations or the movies, a maintenance van is parked outside a dorm, fifty feet away from us. Julie and I spot the van at the same time.

"Either we hijack the van or we show him your badge."

"Both ways will attract attention." Julie states.

"I got a better idea. You start walking towards the library while I divert attention from you guys and walk across the campus." I walk away from the group.

I start walking quickly to the dorm's entrance.

"Let's go professor." Julie grabs her arm again and starts for the library. They have a quick pace to them.

"You do know that his plan won't work right, you cannot get into the building without a swipe key." The Professor states.

Julie and the professor are moving quickly across the wide-open grass towards the library. Jamaica is already in the dorm and the fire alarm is blaring. Jamaica comes out the side entrance closest to the library along with about thirty kids right behind him. He gets swallowed up in the sea of kids.

Jamaica, Julie, and the professor meet at the entrance of the library. There are hundreds of kids swarming around the quad as security shows up to the building.

The professor looks puzzled.

"Don't ask."

Julie looks at Jamaica as she pushes the professor into the library, "Who gave you that key card? I thought only certain agencies had a card that opened most doors."

"When you have friends in high places you can get anything." I offer smugly.

CHAPTER 9

QUIET PLEASE

Phillip and Joe are leaning over the balcony glass railing waiting for us to enter. Joe nods his head for us to follow him upstairs. We head for the stairs and single-file walk up towards Joe. Phillip has arranged chairs in the corner "Study Area" so the five of us can talk and think and hopefully will not be bothered.

Julie is keeping a tight rein on her prisoner. My gut says this woman is no trouble and matter of fact – scared shit.

Forgetting where we are, I start rather loudly, "Let's start with your name."

They all shhh me. "Sorry, name?"

The professor composes herself, looks around knowing someone there recognize her, moves her chair so her back is to anyone coming within our direction.

"Remember, a lot of people know me, plus my picture was plastered all over the campus as a missing person."

"I don't know how much time we have here before we all get noticed, let's have it."

"I was a friend of Mr. Johnson. He knew I had nothing to do with the missing money. This problem all started when your son enrolled at the school. Not many kids get a recommendation letter from a Navy Admiral. We get a lot of kids applying but this raised a flag. Usually, I don't get involved in admissions and neither did Mr. Johnson but this seemed like a "high priority" considering the letter we received, especially since he was not an athlete. We checked into his background and Mr. Johnson figured you might be able to help find the missing money while keeping it quiet."

"You did a background check on my son? Isn't there privacy issues about stuff like that?"

"We Googled you, to be honest, Mr. Biltmore, and found out about your last case."

Feeling proud, "Really?"

"Can we stay on topic here please," Julie begs.

"Mr. Johnson knew he would be blamed for the missing money so he went to the trustees of the school thinking all these upstanding citizens would want to get the authorities involved and that would be the end of it. Well, it turns out all these upstanding citizens went running for the hills with panic."

I am puzzled, to say the least. I don't want to seem lost, but I have no idea who this person is and what role she has in this story. I glance over to Julie who senses there is something wrong. She tugs at my shirt and pulls me over to an empty part of the room.

"You have no idea who this person is, do you?

"I certainly…"

"Johnson mentioned her twice during our meeting with him. He felt she was in danger and something might have happed to her. Look, I know he was droning on and on but you need to pay attention. Can we get back to her story?"

Julie does not wait for me, she heads back to the professor and Phillip. I dutifully follow. I figured I better take over the questioning. Arriving back at the little gathering.

"Why did you go underground?"

"To be honest, Mr. Johnson took me into his confidence awhile back because he was not comfortable with how much this has gotten out of hand. There were a lot of schools getting caught for different violations and being put on probation. On one hand, the publicity for having a championship football team was extremely rewarding. Mr. Johnson got a new contract and big raise and the school received lots of money from the sports departments that let's hire better teachers and grow other sports teams that don't make money which in turn makes us more appealing to other students. This is not so clear cut."

"This doesn't explain you running," Julie asks.

"It seems someone was trying to get Mr. Johnson to turn over the cash otherwise he would be implicated in this mess. They threatened to kill him if he did not cooperate."

There is a moment of silence. Thinking to myself and I figure my cohorts are thinking the same thing – so they stole the money and killed him anyway. This is a mean bunch. I think we better end this and let her get go on her way – wherever that might be.

Julie looks at me, "I guess we are done."

Something strikes me, "we don't know your name, how can we get to you and what are your plans."

She produces a school business card with her cell phone on it. "Call me on the cell, I just decided to leave without telling anyone here, my family has a little beach house in the Keys I think I will hold up there for a bit. My dad is a cop in the town so it's better if I stay close to him."

Julie, Phillip, and Joe start getting up to leave. I must ask, "Two quick questions –Do you know who brought him the cash and why was he chosen to look after it?"

The look on Pamela Winston's face looks like I hit her with a baseball bat. A brief stutter, "Ah, no. He told me about it after it arrived."

Pamela moves away from her chair and heads for the stairs, calling out to her, "Where can I get the list of trustees that Mr. Johnson went to see about the missing money."

Pamela, return to me. Quietly, "Give me your number and I will get you that list."

I hand her my card. She is off, less worried than before, why I have no idea; we were of no help to her.

Pamela walks down the stairs; Phillip looks at me and I nod. He will follow her to make sure she is ok. The day is getting old. Time to regroup and figure out our next move and see if someone reaches out to us. Otherwise, we don't have a client which means no pay, we are in this business to make money.

Chapter 10

Square One

Joe, Julie, and I gather outside the library towards the rear of the building where the loading dock is. Not trying to be too paranoid but if we are standing still talking it's better to be out of sight. Joe's phone goes off.

"We are by the library, more like by the dumpsters, no we are fine.."

Joe looks at me, "Caruso."

Just as he says this, I see Caruso coming through the open quad. From the other end of the quad, I see Phillip walking towards us too. I decide to start with the pleasantries. "How's the move going?"

Caruso will have nothing to do with it, "Are you out of your minds? This is not New York, you are down here what, two days and this is what happens?"

"We just got back down here." Julie grabs my arm.

I see Phillip has something to say, "What?"

Phillip looks at us all, "She was picked up by an unmarked cop car."

"Copeland."

"Copeland," replies Phillip.

Caruso shakes his head, "Tell me what you have."

"What have you got for me?" Everyone looks puzzled except Caruso.

Caruso smirks, reaches under his shirt by the small of his back, and hands me my gun. "This took a lot of called-in favors."

"I'm sure it did. We all appreciate it. Here is the deal…" I drone on and on, not holding anything back.

"Wait a minute, he googled you?" Caruso chuckles. "Talk about feeding the ego. This is incredible. So, there is a slush fund controlled by your dead client to pay athletes at various schools? And the money was funded by major broadcasters, boosters, and advertisers?"

"Since the money is gone and there is nothing written down there is no proof that this occurred," chimes in Julie.

"We do have the lady we were just talking with," offers Joe.

"Unless of course Copeland gets to her first and she talks to some official that buries this information." Phillip worries.

"What's your next move?" Caruso stares at me.

"I'm not sure. Pamela Winston, that lady we just talked with, says she will get me a list of the trustees that Johnson contacted after the money disappeared and ran for hills. One of them must be either behind this mess or at least a small part of it. I would like to get back to the hotel and figure out the next step. Joe, I think you should come back with us, we can get you to class tomorrow."

"I'd rather stay here."

I look at him and the others. Caruso butts in, "I have a few friends looking to make some cash while they figure out what to do down here. Their pension is nice but they are bored stiff. (Chuckle) One certain retired captain opened up a boat rental business with a mob guy who is in the witness protection program. I will ask my buddy to keep an eye. He will stay out of the way. Promise."

We all look at Joe.

"OK, OK." I pat him on the back and we are on our way.

Captain Tom Caruso has been a friend since school days on Long Island. We left high school together, only to join the Navy on the same morning, much to the distress of our parents. We both got lucky and did not see much action except for getting in trouble in as many southern ports as possible.

After our tour of duty was over, we stayed close. He joined the police department, and I worked as an insurance investigator and slowly made my way into this great world of being a P.I since insurance companies no longer had guys like me on the payroll. They felt it would be better to have us as independent contractors. I think it had something to do with their image and ours.

Caruso has saved my ass numerous times with the higher-ups in the police department. He also knows I am kind of a cult hero with the young cops who look for a more exciting life than writing parking tickets and directing traffic at crime scenes.

After all, it was my idea to join the Navy after a futile night of trying to pick up girls at an old crusty Long Island bar named Tabered Ale House.

The idea was to arrive early at the bar so we could at least catch the first wave of girls that came in early. Unfortunately, the night was uneventful as usual. Soon, it was three in the morning, and we had struck out again. Life in Wantagh was boring as hell for us, or so we thought.

The next morning, we fulfilled our beer oath from the night before. When we arrived at the Bethpage recruiting station, completely hungover, the staff sergeant was thrilled to take us. Nobody in their right mind was signing up for the navy in 1972, since the draft was still in effect. The recruitment officer even bought us breakfast. He was going to make his quota for the month.

After being discharged in 1977, life was not much better at home, except we were starting to grow up. Caruso passed the test for the New York City police department, and I got married. A relative got me a job working as an insurance claims investigator, which was as exciting as watching the traffic on the Long Island Expressway on the Fourth of July.

CHAPTER 11

NOW WHAT?

We walk towards the parking lot where our rental car is, was. The long asphalt path winding through the trees is littered with fragments of our dear departed rental car. We were so preoccupied with the going on of the case we forgot about not having a car. From the clearing, we can see fire engines and a few police cruisers still within the area of the charred car.

We all look at the scene than at each other.

"Cab?"

They all look at me as if we have a choice. We head back up the path and towards the other side of campus out towards the stores and restaurants on the other side of a two-lane road. As we start to cross the road, an obvious unmarked car screeches right in front of us followed by a white van.

Copeland!

The window goes down on the unmarked car, Copeland looks at us. "Everyone in," he demands. We stare at him. He peers around me and sees a new figure staring at him. Copeland takes a deep breath, "Captain Caruso I presume?"

Caruso sympathizes with him, "Everyone in." He demands.

Caruso and I take the rear seat of the unmarked car, Julie and Phillip head to the van with the sliding door already open. They disappear into the van.

The driver in his prerequisite cheap suite and dark sunglasses slowly pulls away from the curb. Copeland struggles to turn towards us.

"Ok, this is what I got, two explosions all within hours of your arrival on this quiet campus. One not intended for you, the other intended for you. Obviously, someone is going through a lot of trouble to get rid of you."

I look at him and Caruso, not offering anything.

"Nothing, ok, we have the same information you have. Lots of cash in a safe put there for illegal use in paying football recruits and their families so they have a simple life while playing football for large universities. Some rumors have it that major TV companies might be behind the slush fund, so they get the best and largest audiences watching bowl games while these kids get a few dollars to buy pizza and beer. How's that theory?"

I look at Caruso, "This seems to be an organized system in place which has major universities and major TV networks involved which means there are a lot of asses to protect. This explains the killing of Johnson and the almost killing of us." I stare out the window; the trip seems to have taken us to a remote abandon airfield.

"Where are we headed?" No answer. Copeland looks straight ahead. As we get closer to the hangar, the large sliding plane doors open up and we pull right in. Seems like a government operation. Caruso and I look at each other, "FBI."

Caruso's phone goes off, he listens. "Too late, we are here now."

That gets Copeland's attention who stares at Caruso as he disconnects his call.

"I would venture to say you have a leak," Caruso offers as he opens the door and gets out.

"Shit." Copeland mutters as he too slides out of the car. I can't help but chuckle as does the driver.

Stepping out onto the polished airplane hangar floor from the van is Julie and Phillip. Julie has an - end of a career - look on her face – we spot her boss. She makes her way over to her boss, but he waves her off. This is not good.

James Henderson, all six foot five inches of FBI mass makes his way to us. Either this will go bad or…

"Nice to meet you, Mr. Biltmore," Henderson blurts out extending his meat hoof of a hand. I hear muffled, "oh shits" behind me coming from my cohorts.

"Come this way, please," Henderson turns and leads us into a side office of the main hangar floor. Henderson holds the door open for me and Caruso. He holds his hand up stopping Julie and Phillip from entering the room. Henderson closes the door and the cheap blinds on the door swing violently against the door.

The office has an old metal table and very uncomfortable chairs set up, there are four computers on side desks facing the windowless walls and a through-wall air conditioner banging away endlessly. Henderson walks up to the mini refrigerator in the corner of the room and grabs a bottle of water for himself and points to the refrigerator for us to help ourselves. This is going too smooth for my liking.

"Have a seat."

Caruso grabs a bottle of water for himself and throws one to me as I take a seat at the table.

"Mr. Biltmore, we know the reason you have been called in by Mr. Johnson. We know you had nothing to do with Mr. Johnson's death. We also know someone wants you out of the way. We know you have a wealth of friends like Captain Caruso here. We feel we can help each other."

My head is starting to hurt from his speech pattern.

"Tell me what you know."

I look at Caruso who taps my foot with his and nods towards Henderson.

"I hate to repeat what you already know. I think we no longer have a client who is willing to pay us since he is no longer with us. It looks like this case can be amusing, to say the least, but without getting paid, my associates get cranky. I think we will just wrap up our visit with my son, get in some fishing, and get settled in down here."

Henderson has the look on his face that we have hit a stalemate.

"OK, Mr. Biltmore here is what we will do."

Again, with the 'WE'.

"Here is our offer, Agent Waters will stay on your team and get paid from us while keeping me informed of what you find and if you need help she will be able to reach us. We will cover your cost for yourself and your associates. Captain Caruso here will be compensated by us, through other means. Deal?"

"To be honest, this seems too easy. You could have just threatened us to get lost and you guys could have taken over the case. Why the teamwork, you guys are not known for teamwork."

"You know how Watergate started as a simple break-in and led to a President resigning?"

I nod.

"This may be the Watergate of our time. We are not sure how many people we can trust but we felt that you and your team are the best we have with keeping this out of the news for now."

"How many people above you know about this arrangement?' Caruso inquires.

Henderson gets up from his seat, sticks out his hands to end our meeting.

"Three."

Caruso and I get up, shake his hand and make our way to the door. As I turn the handle of the door, Henderson reaches over me and pushes the door closed.

"One more thing, let's leave Admiral so and so out of this for now. You can trust me for whatever help you need."

Henderson reaches down and opens the door. We walk back out into the hangar.

"Stay in touch, we will drop you back at your new hotel. We gathered your things from the other motel and made it seem like you were busted by the FBI to get whoever is watching you off your tail for now."

Henderson reaches into his pocket and pulls out a phone and calls over Julie.

"Ms. Waters, please." He motions to the room.

Julie walks in first and Henderson closes the door. I see they are standing in front of the door. They are only in there a minute and the door open, Julie appears first holding the phone.

"Thank you, Agent Waters, stay in touch."

"Will do sir," Julie says without looking back at Henderson.

We pile into the van.

I can see Phillip gearing up for the many questions piled up in his head. I give him the not now look and he gets it. Many years of being together help.

"We are being taken to a new hotel. Our stuff was supposedly gathered from our old place and will be dropped to the new place. We will need a new car."

The driver of the van offers up, "There is a new one waiting for you."

"Damn, I need to get back to your son's school to pick up my car.' Laments Caruso. Turning to the driver, "Unless you guys thought of that?"

"No, we did not."

"I can call my son once I know where we are headed, and he can take your car to us. You probably left the keys in the car. Old habits die hard."

Caruso smirks.

We ride in silence through town where we were picked up by Henderson, past the big box stores down a long avenue filled with empty storefronts and many bars and restaurants. The driver turns the van into a 2-star motel parking lot and right around back. He pulls into a spot and hands me 2 sets of keys. They have the room numbers on them.

We all get out of the van. Phillip has a dejected look on his face.

"What did you expect, this is at the government expense." Caruso offers up.

I look at the keys for the room numbers and make my way up the stairwell on the outside of the two-story fake brown stucco motel. I walk down the outside corridor to our room, turn the key, and walk-in. Two stars are being generous. We all walk into one room. The other key is for the room right next door. There is an adjoining door. I guess it's better than one room since there are only three of us. We all look around the room. Phillip takes the other key from my hand, walks outside and into the next room.

"In here."

Phillip opens his side of the adjoining door and Julie opens up our side. Looking into where Phillip is standing, I see three large, FBI evidence bags piled up on the beds. I must give them credit for keeping the ruse up.

Caruso picks up a flyer from the desk and pulls out his cell phone. "Hey, how are things going? I know we have been busy. We will explain when you get here. My car is parked in the lot behind the library. A White Ford Explorer, keys in the cupholder. We are at Sunset Motel, 4344 Hemingway Ave. GPS is pretty good in the car. See you in about 15."

Caruso hangs up the phone. "Your son is on his way."

CHAPTER 12

JUST START TALKING

Caruso closes the door but opens the blinds to let in some light. He stands next to the window peering out watching for something. It takes me a second to realize that he is keeping an eye out for Joe. I take my phone out and dial…… no answer. Shit. Caruso points out the window as Joe pulls into the parking lot with Caruso's rental car. He knew my concern.

Caruso opens the door to the room to wave Joe in. As we wait for Joe to climb the stairs it gives me time to think of our next move. Phillip meets Joe at the door to our room. I stare at them as they enter – I got nothing. I have no friggin idea what we are supposed to do next. I do not know who we should contact, who our client is besides the US government and I have no idea where to get started. Everyone who has half a brain and follows college sports knows this shit has been going on for years, maybe not to the extreme that has transpired over the last day but there is a lot of money involved, millions, heck maybe even billions.

Everyone is staring at me for leadership or at least a clue as to where we can eat dinner. I'm speechless. Caruso notices my nonverbal communication.

"Phillip, let's you and I go grab some food and some beer and we will eat in. Julie why don't you try and get him to talk out a plan while we are gone. I know this guy for 30 years and I never heard this type of silence from him."

Caruso and Phillip leave the room. I do what I do best, I pace.

"How long has he been like this?" Joe looks at Julie.

Julie stares, "Ever since we got back."

"Dad?"

"I got nothing. I have no clue where to go or who to see. You two have any ideas?"

Julie looks at me, "These people are money criminals though they probably do not realize it. They most likely hired someone to take care of Johnson never dreaming that these guys would kill him. This business has been going on for so long and has morphed into a business that has engrossed our entire nation and into the fabric of our daily lives. The only thing bigger is the business it leads to – the betting that takes place on these games. I'm not sure even the FBI is big enough to bring it down. Look we all know that this has been going on forever, and no one has been able to get someone to talk about it?"

"She is right Dad. Just because some college president gets blown up do we think our little band of private eyes can bring down an institution like college sports?"

"It's not about bringing down college sports, I'd like to think it's about the little athlete that gets recruited to a big-time school that he cannot afford to go to. His parents get some needed cash and the kid thinks he is the next Brett Favre and is treated like a god on campus, good for him. But then on day three he blows out his knee, his scholarship gets taken away from him, the money to the parents dries up and the kid either takes out a loan to stay in school or goes home because he did not belong there in the first place. The so-called boosters do not give a shit about this kid only about watching their beloved college team win some stupid bowl game to make their lives better."

Caruso and Phillip walk in as the rant finishes. I stare at them.

"Maybe our case is that we are trying to stop these nuts from killing again and maybe, just maybe we shed some light on a system that has grown bigger than anyone ever imagined."

"Not to spoil our pep talk but has anyone wondered why Copeland did not want our navy buddy involved? Caruso looks around, opens the food bag, and pulls out a fry, "Just wondering."

Just as Caruso finishes there is a knock on the door. We all pause a second then Caruso slowly opens the door. Once a cop always a cop. Thank God.

"I'm looking for Jamaica Biltmore. I'm Frank Stein, head legal counsel for the NCAA. Can I come in?"

Caruso opens the door to let our visitor in. Frank Stein is a well-appointed man of fifty or so. Mr. Stein is a very expensive suit figuratively speaking. Like always with us, the hotel room is very cramped.

"Does everyone need to be here for this?" wonders Stein.

"I prefer that they stay. I'm not sure I will remember and or believe this conversation ever took place." This seems to go over Stein's head.

Stein reaches into the inside pocket of his suit and pulls out an envelope and hands it over. I figured I do not have to read it if he is going to explain it anyway. I hand it to Julie. "This is a request by the NCAA to discontinue your investigation since we are running an investigation of our own and we would not want to hamper what we are looking into."

"What exactly are you looking into?"

"It's hard to say."

"Give it a try."

"We are looking into a call from President Johnson. He called and said there was some missing money, maybe from the bowl game they recently won. We have no knowledge of this behavior in the past and we are taken back by the allegations that some people in certain quarters are stating."

Oh good, legal speak. Wonder where he got the idea of the –CASH.

Phillip cannot help but jump in, "Are you trying to say that this is the first instance that the NCAA has heard of cash payments to athletes? Don't you guys subscribe to Sports Illustrated?"

Stein shuffles from one foot to the other while staying calm.

"Look, we are asking that you suspend any further investigation. We will handle it internally with our security forces. We are well equipped to handle these cases."

Now it's Caruso's turn, "You guys are equipped to handle murder cases too?"

Stein turns to Caruso, " We are not sure what President Johnson was up to. We prefer to let the police handle that. I see that I have taken up enough of your time. If you have any questions my number is on the letter in the envelope. Have a nice day."

With that Stein heads for the door.

I have one last question, "How did you know how to find us?"

Stein turns, "We all know people Mr. Biltmore. Good day."

Stein walks out and Caruso holds the door for a second then closes the door behind him. Caruso suddenly opens the door and steps out of the room. Knowing something has caught his attention, we all follow.

Chapter 13

The Envelope Please

From our luxury accommodations, we watch as Mr. Stein stops on the way to his car in the parking lot. He spots Pamela Winston walking from the far end of the parking lot towards the stairs leading to our room.

"How....

Before I can finish, "I called her cell to tell her where we are staying just in case she finds that list we need." Julie jumps in.

Pamela is walking quickly towards the stairs with a large brown envelope in her hand. Stein looks on with a puzzled look. If he approached her as if he knew her I would have packed my bags and went home. That would be a turn of events I could not buy into. Stein gets into his car and drives off. We all head back into the room, the very crowded room. By the time we make our way back inside, Pamela is at the door. We need to get a bigger room for these meetings.

Pamela walks in and hands Caruso the envelope.

"That was quick", is all I got.

"I spoke with my Dad, he is on his way up here but said I should turn this over to you now."

Caruso opens the envelope, scans it, and hands it to me, I hand it to Julie.

"Mr. Biltmore, you need to understand that these college towns' entire economic life revolves around sports. Every person who owns a small business can sustain their entire year of slow business only because of the few home football games and basketball games. Without these games, these towns become a blight on the state." Pamela turns to walk out after her speech.

"I get it, but all this money is made on the backs of the athletes who do not get a cent, and all those hundreds of volunteers who get a tee shirt as pay after working a game. These kids get a few bucks for meals, or they get someone to do their reports for them does not justify any of this…. just my opinion."

Pamela nods and walks out; my gang has their mouths open so wide I could drive a semi into them.

"I had a friend of mine who worked as a volunteer for the US Open a few years ago on Long Island. He was retired and had time on his hands thinking working at the event would be cool. He worked seven miles from the event directing traffic." I start.

"Not everyone can work on the course, that's a crapshoot." Chimes in my son.

"He had to pay to volunteer!" I finish my rant. "Let's get some air," I lead us out of the stuffy room and into the sunshine. That feels good.

"OK, looking at the list, it has names and a few addresses but otherwise how do we track down these people?" Julie says trying to get us back on track.

We walk down the stairs with our food in hand. Caruso points to a broken-down picnic table under a scrub pine off the parking lot.

CHAPTER 14

NOWHERE TO GO

We spend a few minutes in silence finishing our cold lunch. I got nothing. Phillip is standing against an old pine tree drinking his cold coffee. I look at everyone, back and forth.

Oh well, I better start, "Besides a destroyed rental car, what else do we have here, and do we need to stay involved?"

Now everyone has taken up my dumb stare and looks back and forth at each other.

"I can head back to my house and get some fishing in, I guess," Caruso offers up.

Boy, that sounded like a disappointed little kid whose little league game got canceled.

"I might take a drive down the coast, enjoy the sun," Phillip joins in.

"I guess I can go to class, this will blow over I am sure," Joe jumps in.

I look at Julie who shrugs.

"I guess we can call Copeland and tell him since we have no client per se we are off the case." I am looking for validation here from the bored team.

"I'll handle Copeland, I can drive Joe back to campus and take Phillip where he wants to go," Caruso gets up and starts dialing his phone. Phillip nods and heads for the room to grab his stuff.

"Jamaica, I will be at the Ritz in Palm Beach. When you feel like it come down and join me, we could use the break."

Phillip and I met while I was in the insurance business. He knew every scheme possible in fraud claims. He was a natural crook, who also happens to be a great mystery writer when he feels like it. I was introduced to him when I was working on a stolen car ring and my case took me to Jamaica. Caruso, who was becoming a rising star in the police department, gave me Phillip's name as a possible lead, or at least a person who might know something of value in the case.

The fact of the matter was that Phillip had family ties on some of the islands and had fished at all the remote ports since he was a kid. He made enough money on some early books he had written to allow him the time and money to do as he pleased now.

This lack of occupation led the police to keep a close eye on him until Caruso finally came on one of our many fishing trips and realized the police were being led on a wild goose chase by a mystery writer whose fish stories were part of his life. Phillip loved the ruse.

"You OK with going back to school?" I ask worriedly.

"I will be fine."

"I just spoke with Copeland. He is keeping a few guys at the school. He wants Joe to check with him when he gets back. Copeland will get it out that you are off the case. This should take the heat off Joe and the rest of us. I will check in later. You and Julie can come down for dinner."

Within ten minutes our merry group has disbanded. Julie and I head to the room to pack up and figure out where to go next. I go to the front office to pay our bill for the few hours we are here. This motel sucks. I walk to the rental car to open it up so it's not so hot when I barely notice the convertible corvette pulling off the highway and into the parking lot. There is no one in the passenger seat so I know it's not a quickie he is coming here for.

Julie is down the stairs headed to the car when she too spots the car. Her antenna is better than mine, but I still feel this car does not belong here. The car pulls slowly towards me. Julie has that FBI look on her face, she reaches into my bag for my gun. She is close enough to see the guy is smiling at me.

"Mr. Biltmore, Jilly Ricardo. I have an invitation for you to join Mr. Farante for drinks at his club this afternoon."

"Why would I want to join him and how does he know me, I do not know his name."

"He knows of your reputation; he has some information regarding some missing money. It's a nice place, public if you know what I mean," offers the hulk in the nice car. "Oh, bring your friend, the dress is golf casual.

56

Maybe you hit a few while you are there." I take the envelope from Jilly.

Jilly turns the car around and heads out of the lot.

"What the hell was that about and how did he know to find us here?"

I open the envelope and read it. "The club is about twenty minutes from here. Drinks at 4. We have an hour. Thoughts?"

Julie throws the bag in the car, "Does it say who we are meeting?"

"The big guy said Mr. Farante." I get in the car.

Julie looks through the bag for the envelope that Caruso left. She has a blank look on her face. "His name is not on this list. Do we think the club will be a safe place to go?"

All I can think about is Odd Job throwing his hat and knocking the head off the statue; Bond -What will the club secretary say? Goldfinger – Oh nothing Mr. Bond, I own the club.

"I think we will be OK."

CHAPTER 15

BABY YOU CAN DRIVE MY CAR

We pull out of the parking lot.

"Where are we headed."

I look over at Julie, "Shopping?"

Julie smiles and sinks into the seat. A relaxed look comes to her face.

We are barely out of the driveway and onto the highway when a familiar sedan swings into our lane and stops right in front of us. I jam on the brakes, not because I do not want to ram the idiot in front of me, it's the thought of ruining another rental car. I'll lose all my points.

As I slowly open the door of the car, Julie has one hand on the door handle and one hand in the bag in the back seat fumbling for a gun. We both notice Copeland getting out of his driver's side door while the seat belt is still around his bulk. I cannot help but chuckle. There is no need to get out of the car now. Looking in the rearview mirror cars are piling up behind us. I hit the window button and crock my head out the window, " Can we pull off the road and chat?"

Copeland smirks and gets back into his car and jerks his car forward and pulls ahead of us into the coffee shop parking lot.

"What the ...." Julie says with a pissed-off voice.

I throw the car in drive and follow into the coffee shop. Cars speed around us waving their middle finger at us. I take it that this is for Copeland and not us. It makes me feel better.

CHAPTER 16

DECAF PLEASE.

Copeland is standing next to his car as we pull in. I motion to Julie to stay put. I bounce out of the car, "Can I get you a coffee?"

Julie looks confounded, "Coffee?"

I cannot wait for the answer, I will get her an iced coffee, and it will make her feel better. I leave the door open a bit. Copeland looks to start talking before I even get to him.

"I have come with a warning, this meeting with Farante comes with a lot of unknowns."

There is no way they look of surprise is not a billboard across my face. "How did you...." I really can't continue such a stupid question.

"We are not sure who this guy is, every time we think we have good intel on him it seems to take a different turn. If you come up with something, I would appreciate a heads up." Copeland does not wait for an answer, he gets back in his car and drives around the building and out again onto the highway. I look over at Julie and point to the coffee shop. Julie shakes her head no and points to her watch. I agree, not a time for coffee, time for the golf club. I head for the car and get in.

Julie has the look of – What the f…. was that all about.

I start the car and pull around the coffee shop and back on the highway.

"We have been warned about this meeting. This Farante guy seems to be on everyone's radar but they have no idea who or what he is. Do me a favor, look at the invite and plug the address into your phone and find out where we are going."

Julie looks at me, "We have a lot of connections across many avenues, don't you think we can make a few calls and find out who this guy is?"

Excitedly, "I was thinking we would try and guess first."

"Jesus, make a left at the next light. The club is up 3 miles on the right."

"Do you think we are dressed ok?"

Julie looks at me and down at her clothes. "We are fine."

We pull into the exceptionally long tree-lined driveway of the golf club. The signs state, PRIVATE, the greenery says high initiation fee. The highway we just pulled off was brown and dry, we have landed in OZ. At the end of the driveway is a sprawling adobe-colored clay barrel roof clubhouse fronted by a circular driveway. We are waved to the front entrance by a young blond-haired skinny kid dressed in the uniform of all the other hired help – and me. Khakis and a dark blue polo. Mine is untucked so there. Julie and I get out of the car. We are directed around the side of the clubhouse.

We walk in silence around the clubhouse, past the open veranda, whatever a veranda is, past the putting green which seems silly actually, and towards the outdoor dining area and the hostess. She lifts her head from the reservation book in front of her and smiles too nicely.

"You are here for Mr. Farante? Please follow me."

We are led to a table in the corner of the planter encircled dining area. Mr. Farante I presume stands when he sees us coming. Small and compact, very Peter Faulk like more on that later, dressed in yellow and blue golf clothes. In the distance I see my good friend Jilly chatting with two older men on the first tee. We are waved to sit down. A waitress comes over, "Can we get you something to drink?"

"Iced tea for me," Julie says.

"I'll have a beer, Heineken" I look at Mr. Farante who is drinking coffee.

"Mr. Biltmore, nice to see you out of New York, the weather here is so much better don't you thinks so?"

"Miss Waters, please order what you like, Mr. Biltmore?"

"Please order me a turkey club. I will be right back."

I get up from the table and follow Farante out of the dining area and towards the first tee. He is holding a putter. I don't get it.

"Do you play Mr. Biltmore?"

"No, I guess I never had time. I thought once I retired, I would take it up."

"Any time you would like to give it a try I'd be happy to help. Let's go this way."

Farante leads us away from the first tee, the sign says the first tee, otherwise, I would have no idea what that means. It's a silly game. We stop at a small gazebo off the path, what a great wedding photo location. I need to get to the bottom of why we are here. I am just not sure this conversation will offer up any clues. I look back at Julie who is engaged in a deep conversation with Jilly.

"Mr. Biltmore, I have been following the news of the late president of our esteemed University and I have gotten word from some friends about a safe and a lot of missing money. Some very nervous friends have an interest…."

He is a wealthy donor that is scared shit.

"… in the return of the money. We would like to find and bring to justice….

No donor, someone in the legal field.

"… You need to understand, I have no jurisdiction here but the people in our company….

Oh Shit, the CIA. I look at Julie. She has the 'oh shit look' on her face.

"… take my card, please whatever you hear, I am just looking for some help. I have some contacts that could help with technical issues during your investigation."

"I have no client, so we are dropping this." He does not need to know about the FBI fronting us some money.

"Do not drop this so quickly. You never know when a client will appear." Farante sticks out one hand to shake and the other he hands me the putter. "I have a tee time in 15, enjoy your lunch. When you are done, try putting, it might grab you. It usually does." Farante turns and walks away leaving me holding my new putter. There are just so many responses I have spinning around in my head that none come out as Farante walks towards the first tee. I head back to Julie sitting by herself at the lunch table.

I walk past the hostess who turns to me, "Mr. Farante said to please have lunch on him."

"Thank you."

I pull my chair out and a waiter hands me my cloth napkin. "Let me get you a new order of fries, these must be cold by now."

I lean my new putter against the table.

The waiter takes my plate and I stare at Julie who is head down in her salad. She lifts her head as the waiter disappears.

"CIA" we both whisper at the same time.

"What the fuck?" Is all I got.

"Have all your cases touched every branch of law enforcement or am I just getting lucky with the last two?" Julie kind of accuses me of something, but I don't know what. "And what's with the putter."

"He thinks it will get me hooked on golf."

"I have learned when cases involve missing money, and I mean a lot of money, everyone is involved. This is more exciting than a cheating husband."

The waiter comes back with my warm plate as Jilly walks back to the table. He pulls out a chair and sits down. The waiter brings him a beer without him asking, that's service.

"Mr. Farante wants to make it clear that he thinks though there are missing links to the disappearing money, they are not all connected, at least as far as he is concerned. He wants to level with you, he could use your help, there are certain things he cannot do. He would appreciate it if you contact me if you feel the money trail starts picking up steam." With that Jilly gets up and sticks out his hand. We shake and he follows up with the same to Julie. He grabs his beer and heads away. He stops and turns.

"You'll like it down here. Your kid will like school too. Mine did. We will keep an extra eye on him too." Jilly shakes his head and walks back to the table.

"I almost forgot." He reaches into his back pocket and hands me an envelope. "We realize you do not have a client any longer, so Mr. Farante wants to keep you on a retainer, this should help."

I take the envelope and Jilly walks again, finally for good. I must look. It's a cashier's check made out to me from a local big bank for ten thousand dollars. I hand it to Julie.

"Finally, some money. Sorry, kidding. Thoughts?"

"A lot." I take some fries, "Ready to go?" I take a twenty from my pocket and leave it as the tip. I can be generous with a large check in my hand. Julie takes a large gulp of her iced tea and we both get up and walk towards the front of the clubhouse in silence. I swing my new club back smacking it against a light pole. Julie shakes her head. I hand the preppy car attendant my ticket. He runs off to get to my car. My car is pulled in front of the clubhouse in a matter of minutes. In New York one time, they could not find my car for an hour... I drove a convertible Corvette. I guess they had to wait for the friend to come back from a joy ride.

We get in. I throw my new golf club into the back seat. Julie pulls out her phone. She dials, "Hi, can you do me a favor and do a quick check on a Mr. Farante, no, we know nothing more about him. I can send a picture. Great, talk soon."

"A picture, how did that happen?"

"When you and Farante went for your walk and Jilly left the table. I made it look like I was taking a picture of the golf course. I had a feeling we would need it."

"Pretty sharp. You are a lot smarter than I seem to be."

CHAPTER 17

A JOY RIDE

It's not what you think, keep reading.

"I'm not sure who we should call first." As my phone rings. I fumble with it and look at the number and hand it to Julie.

Julie looks at the number and answers it. "Hey Joe, your dad is driving, what's up."

I keep looking at Julie as she nods her head to a conversation I cannot hear, actually it's not much of a conversation since Joe seems to be the only one talking.

"Ok, we will head over there, keep an eye out. We think we know what that's all about." Julie presses end and places the phone in the cupholder.

"He thinks someone is following him. I tend to believe him, his instincts are pretty good. I think we should head over."

"I agree." I step on the gas. My anxiety level seems to go up as I drive closer to the school.

"Since we moved out of that dive motel we have no place to stay. We can go to Caruso's place or catch up with Phillip at the Ritz." Julie offers up to calm me down.

"Caruso and his Sarah probably could use the alone time; I think the Ritz it is. Please text Phillip and see if he can get us a room. Maybe even pay."

Julie slaps my arm as her phone rings, "Hey Joy, you got hit this quickly?"

Another one-way conversation.

"Ok got it, thanks for trying. Speak soon."

"Well?"

"My friend at the local bureau office says this guy, Farante or whoever he is has a locked file."

"Would you normally lock a file if the person is a worker in another agency?"

"Yes, if this person is classified."

"Humm."

I pull into the parking lot where our previous rental car is still a pile of shredded metal in a heap.. I figure what are the chances of our second car getting….. probably pretty good from my luck. My phone sounds a tapping sound – a text from Joe.

I pick up the phone, he's in the gym watching a girls' volleyball game. We get out of the car and head for the gym across the massive lawn. It's starting to get dark. I make an awkward turn back towards the car and to the driver's side door. Julie looks at me and nods towards her purse. She took my gun. Is she perfect or what?

CHAPTER 18

METAL DETECTOR

Tap, Tap, another text. He's on the bleachers under the green basketball banners. Julie and I approach the gym doors.

"Do you think they have….." I start.

She finishes, "Metal detectors? Yes, they do."

We walk up to the college kid manning the entrance desk. He has an open box and is looking for 5 bucks each to come in. Julie takes out a ten and her FBI badge.

"I'd rather the detector not go off."

"Is there a problem, shall I call security?" The frightened kid stammers.

"Not unless we are losing, my niece, is on the team."

I swear I saw the bead of sweat recede into the hair.

Julie hands him her bag and he hands it back to her around the detector.

"Please do not tell anyone I did that."

"No worries, what could happen at a volleyball game," I state with utter confidence which is probably a mistake.

Not wanting to spook anyone, I motion to Julie for us to take seats on the opposite side of the gym from Joe. I can tell he sees us. Another text.

Quietly, "He says the guy is in the stands at the far end of the bleachers on the same side as him."

A loud cheer erupts and I hear people walking down the plastic bleachers which sounds like a rumbling thunderstorm coming closer. A swell of people is taking advantage of the break-in action.

Tap, Tap.

Joe has lost full contact but sees a very large man mixing with the crowd.

Julie and I don't bother to sit down. We start scanning the crowd while keeping an eye on Joe who seems frozen in his seat. I guess better to keep low.

Julie just heads into the crowd, it's a damn volleyball game, and the place is packed. In high school, the only people who showed up for volleyball games were the parents of the players and the so-called boyfriends. There is an ESPN table set up.

I keep an eye on Joe, some fans around him are standing and stretching their legs waiting for the next game to start. I see a large guy headed up the bleachers.

"Julie…" I call over the loud crowd.

Joe sees the guy coming for him. I run through the crowd. Julie catches me as I grab her purse.

"It's Jilly."

I notice Jilly gets to Joe as he sticks his hand out to, I guess, introduce himself, at least I hope that is what he's doing.

We are now close enough for Joe to point us out and Jilly waves. Out of the right side of the bleachers, two guys crash into Jilly. Jilly braces himself and pushes Joe out of the way. Julie and I are within reach of the mayhem that is about to ensue. Joe jumps on one of the guys who is trying to get to him.

Julie throws one guy from the bleachers and pins him down. We have a big crowd gasping in shock. The second guy is being held by Jilly and Joe.

"Hello, Jilly."

"Dad, you know him?"

"We do."

Security has shown up in droves. The campus police are arriving as well. The crowd and the teams have retreated to a safe part of the gym. Three of the policemen are standing over Julie with guns drawn.

She looks over her shoulder, "ID is in the bag, FBI."

Jilly shoots me a look with super-wide eyes. I am figuring he does not want to be here. One of the cops looks at me.

"I know you; you were here during the explosion episode in the president's office."

I hope this is not going to be an issue.

"Let's get everyone outside, Agent…." The cop asks.

"Waters."

"My guys will take this guy out of here. Who is the other guy?" The officer points to Jilly.

"I think he's just a guy in the stands who saw these guys coming to my son." I lean to shake Jilly's hand. "Thanks for helping sir." Jilly shakes back and slowly walks away.

To keep up the ruse, I turn to Joe, "Did you say something to piss off these two guys, maybe Joe said something to one of the girls and one of these guys is her father."

Joe, Julie, and I follow the officers and the two men out of the gym. Bursting through the outside double doors is no other than Copeland.

Great, another tall story we need to come up with.

Outside the gym, there are five security and campus police cars plus Copeland's car encircling the gym entrance.

"So you two just happened to be showing up at a volleyball game when these two clowns decide to attack your son?"

"Thank God we did. Otherwise...."

"Son, anything to add?" Turning to Joe.

"I texted my dad, I felt like I was being followed. It's that simple."

Trying to get the conversation back to the two guys, "I would appreciate it if you would let me know who these guys might be. You said to keep an eye out."

Copeland shakes his head, "This is getting bigger Mr. Biltmore. If someone is brazened enough to try and grab your son during an event in the gym......."

I was going to interrupt and question his choice of words, *event* ... but I thought better of it.

".…. obviously, they are trying to get to you. I thought you didn't have a client anymore?"

"We don't, but now I don't need one." I grab Julie and Joe by the arm and walk past the army of security guards.

"Mr. Biltmore.... this is not over."

Turning over my shoulder, "*You are right, a nice show of force, next time let's get there before I need to step in. This is twice you are the last one to the party.*"

Julie now grabs my arm to get me out of there before I say aloud what I was thinking. Those previously things said over my shoulder were said in my head. One of these days.

Julie, Joe, and I head away from the gym, down a path towards Joe's dorm. We really can find our way around this campus. I notice Jilly coming from another direction towards us. I notice Copeland staring at us; I do not want Jilly to walk up to us. I try and warn him with my eyes. Sounds silly but I see it work in the movies. Jilly stops in his track, pulls out his phone, and starts talking, or at least he pretends to be talking. I guess my warning worked.

We keep walking towards the dorm and out of sight from Copeland. Julie looks back, "Copeland is gone."

Jilly sees what Julie has seen and walks over to us.

"Nice warning, I noticed the eye roll."

"Let's keep walking." I put my hand on Jilly's back and nudge him toward a more remote location.

Joe leads us to his dorm; he opens the door with his passkey. As we follow him he leads us to a study area on the first floor next to the laundry room. We close the door, I don't feel like going around and around with chit-chat.

"Jilly, tell me why is the CIA involved with missing money from a college bowl game and a blown-up college president? I thought the CIA only had jurisdiction out of the country?"

Jilly is shaking his head, no, and putting his hands up.

"Who says CIA?"

Julie looks at him with laser eyes. It's creepy.

"I work for Mr. Farante. We were hired to help a few of the boosters track down the missing money. What Mr. Farante does in his spare time is his business. These are good friends. His check that you took means you are working for him and the boosters."

I look over at Julie and Joe. I hate well-thought-out reasoning.

"What is your next step, Mr. Biltmore?"

"Why would the NCAA come talk with me?"

Jilly frowns and turns around to pace the room, "Who came to see you, Mr. Stein?"

"How did...." Joe asks in amazement.

"Is he not from NCAA?" Julie asks.

"More like from the Southern Football Conference, kind of like the same as the NCAA. Mr. Biltmore, every time Sports Illustrated does an expose on some kid's family getting cash to help them survive the news grabs a hold of it and everyone loses their mind."

"Yeah, but it blows over by the time the next magazine comes out. Let's take the blowing up of the late President Johnson, what makes this case different than any other underground funds for college athletes" I question.

"There needs to be some connection between President Johnson and...."

I interrupt Joe, "Maybe the money missing from the safe had nothing to do with football and the boosters."

If I could use a cliché more than I normally do, Jilly looks like he ate the canary and the entire cage.

"Jilly, where do you operate out of? Can we chat with Farante?"

Julie walks away from the conversation and makes a call.

Jilly heads for the door, "You have my number, and I will speak with Mr. Farante to try and set up a meeting."

Jilly leaves.

"I'm not happy with the thought of you staying in this place. Someone is trying to get to you. This was remarkably close, if not for Jilly…." I know I have a cockeyed look on my face.

"What?" Julie asks.

"I guess I am suspicious about everyone. I know Jilly said he would look after Joe, but the timing seems…."

"Incredible?" Julie remarks.

"Who did you call?" I enquire.

"Caruso and Phillip, time to get the band back together. We got a payment; let's put it to good use." Julie offers as she walks out of the room.

"Joe, grab some stuff and meet us back down here. No objections."

"I'm not going to fight you on this. That was a bit unsettling. Give me five minutes."

Joe heads for the elevator, I cannot help myself, I trot after him, sticking my hand into the elevator door as it starts to close causing the door to open back up. Joe has a smirk on his face.

"What took you so long."

We ride up in silence, facing the door.

Without looking at Joe, "This is pretty exciting, right?"

All I hear is a muffled chuckle. "All that's missing is a bar to hang out in."

I turn, "You know something you're right, that would be great, especially on the water."

The door opens and we get out and walk towards his room. Joe opens his doors, we walk in.

"Ever think about retiring dad?"

"All the time, there are a few hold-ups, one big thing, making enough money to enjoy life a bit. You'll go on your way eventually and it would be nice to be settled. You could be working cases, I could consult when you get into a tight fix, for a good fee of course."

"That goes without saying." Joe finishes throwing a few things in his bag. We turn to leave, and Julie is by the door.

"Caruso will meet us at the Ritz for drinks at 7. He's going to dinner with his wife. Phillip got us a couple of rooms."

We walk out of the room, Joe locks up behind us and we head for the elevator.

"And?" Julie looks at me.

And?" I reply.

Julie laughs," Henderson thinks Farante is CIA but freelancing. He probably uses his CIA ID to get through many doors. It's not very legal, but he has a good rep. Very loyal standup guy, if he makes a little side money no one cares."

We get into the elevator.

"What about Copeland." I offer up.

"Too obvious."

Julie and I look at Joe.

"Joe is right, using his federal marshal office without hiding it would be crazy if he is mixed up in this."

"Something seems wrong."

The elevator door opens, and we walk out of the dorm towards our car. I am not in the mood for another car issue. We walk in silence towards the parking lot. Everyone looks shady. Julie reaches down and grabs my hand. She looks me in the eye and nods towards Joe who is walking in front of us. I do notice his head spinning around like Linda Blair in the Exorcist.

I reach out and put my hand on Joe's shoulder.

"You ok buddy?"

"Yeah, great, just trying to keep an eye out for bad guys. Everything that has happened to us during this case seems to happen while we are on campus.

"He's got a point."

I hold onto Julie a bit tighter until we walk into the parking lot and towards our car.

As if on cue, I hear screeching tires come blasting into the lot. Julie lets go and grabs for her bag. Joe moves behind a large SUV. I just shake my head as I notice the all too familiar convertible, come slamming to a stop in front of us.

"I want to thank you for helping out back there earlier."

"No problem Jilly. Do you have any idea what that show of force was all about in the gym?"

"Where are you three-headed?"

"Just to crash for the night. We figured we'd get a start early and try and piece this thing together. We have a bunch of little loose ends but we are having trouble tying them together."

Julie looks at me, I know what she is thinking.

Jilly pauses, all I can think of is ...please do not ask, please do not ask, please do not ask. "OK, I'll call you in the morning. Mr. Farante has ideas he wants to run past you."

"Have a good night Jilly."

"You thought he was going to ask us where we were staying didn't you." Julie laughs and heads for the car.

"It never crossed my mind." I unlock the doors, Joe gets in the back and motions for Julie to take the front.

We get in the car, "And that babbling on and on without actually saying anything was priceless."

I proudly turn to Julie, "Thanks."

CHAPTER 19

SILENCE

We ride in silence down the coast for twenty minutes towards our new digs. I think everyone is a bit tired. We haven't had much rest since we started this. I can see Joe nodding off in the rearview mirror. Julie also seems to be closing her eyes. She rests her hand on mine on the center console.

My phone, which is sitting in the cup holder, goes off like a three-alarm fire siren. Julie jumps, but Joe stays asleep.

I pick up the phone to talk, no hands-free, no blue tooth, talking the old fashion way. I must, I recognized the number.

All I can do is listen, Julie stares at me.

Finally, I get to speak, "The Ritz, don't be a wise ass. Seven sounds good, in the bar." I hit the send button and put the phone back down.

I turn to Julie, "Bill."

This wakes up a groggy Joe from the back seat.

"Uncle Bill?"

"Yup, he'll meet us for drinks at seven."

"You're in trouble…" Julie laughs teasingly as she closes her eyes for the rest of the trip.

Joe is back asleep, and Julie is right behind him.

CHAPTER 20

A SHOT IN THE DARK

We arrive at the Ritz, the name a fitting description of the enormous hotel. Of course, it has valet parking, when have we stopped being able to park our cars.

"We're here." I don't wait for the sleepy heads to awake; I open the trunk and get out our bags for Julie and me.

Another valet has shown up with a luggage cart. (I am not going into this.)

Julie and Joe get out of the car and slowly make their way up the steps of the hotel. Now, this is a hotel. The grounds are manicured to perfection. The help is dressed better than most Wall Street guys, and I am sure what we are paying for a room more than covers it. You need to give Phillip credit for this place. Another valet opens the door. I shake my head, "Thank you."

Julie, Joe, and I head to the check-in desk.

"Mr. Biltmore?" A perky receptionist asks.

Being recognized always cheers me up.

"Mr. Meli just came by when he saw you pull up. We have a room for you and Ms. Waters and one for your son."

The clerk hands us the keys. Nothing to sign, very impressive, it's about time Phillip takes care of something, the freeloader.

"Mr. Meli gave us your contact information and a credit card to hold the three rooms; he said you will take care of the bill when you check out."

"Of course, he did. What a …."

Julie grabs my arm and pulls me away. Joe is already at the elevator. I look at my watch, 6:00. We ride up in silence. The elevator is nicer than my first apartment, even bigger.

"Joe, come to our room at six-fifty."

Joe takes a key from my hand and looks at our room number.

"OK."

The door opens on the sixth floor. We part ways. I make sure Joe gets to his room and he gets in alone. I'm in no mood for any drama right now. Julie and I get to our room. We never really talked about this. I start to open the door and stop.

"We never talked about this; I can go get another room since I seem to pay for all of them anyway. The other motel we kind of got placed together since the FBI only got us two rooms."

Julie grabs my hand and walks me into the room. This is a lot better than the motel we were at a few hours ago. Alone at last. I drop our bags; I walk slowly to Julie who is admiring the view of the lush grounds of the hotel.

I turn her around, "I know we said to take this slow but…"

There is a loud knock at the door.

"This can't be going any slower," is what I think she just said. I roll my eyes and head for the pounding. I turn to Julie, "Any guesses?"

I decide to play it smart and look through the peephole. Phillip.

I open the door.

"Can we help you?"

Phillip walks in past me. "I made some calls after I settled in a few hours ago. I have a few friends who like to gamble on college football games. It seems some mid-sized bookies are having a hard time laying off their larger bets."

I close the door.

Julie looks puzzled.

I figured I would take a shot at this. I need to sit down though. I sit on the couch and Julie sits in the chair by the window. Phillip looks back and forth at us.

"You two look very tired."

I ignore him, "See, if the bookie is tied into a large organization, he takes bets from his customers, when the action gets too big he needs to lay off the bets – in other words, get a larger bookie to help him cover the potential payouts. This goes up the ladder as the payoff becomes potentially very large. It's like a pyramid."

"It's kind of like insurance companies going to a re-insurance company to help them with potential large claims." Julie chimes in.

"Sure, I guess so." I never heard of such a thing. It makes a lot of sense. Back on track.

"So?"

"It seems that maybe, just maybe, the missing ten million dollars is out there somewhere and might have been used for other illegal purposes."

"I have heard that college football and professional football betting is in the hundreds of millions of dollars."

Phillip nods, "Good point."

I get up and escort him out of the room.

"We need to get a bit of rest. See you at seven in the bar."

I close the door. Julie has moved onto the bed. To add to the ongoing cliché of the story, this is where the screen would go black, and when it opens up, we would be showered, dressed, and heading out for our seven o'clock drinks.

CHAPTER 21

MIND YOUR OWN BUSINESS

Julie and I are showered and dressed. (I told you so.) There is a knock at the door. I open the door to see Joe looking awake. I close the door as we head to the lobby bar.

"What do you think this case is all about Dad?"

"It is starting to feel a lot like the last case, gamblers, government agencies, and lots of missing cash."

"Maybe we need to expand our marketing, how many cases can there be that involve all these shady characters?"

I look at Julie, sarcasm is not what I was expecting, but from her it is cute.

The elevator empties into the lobby, the bar is in the far end of the massive lobby. I see Caruso and Phillip sitting at a table in the corner by the large window looking out over the pool area. We walk over to the table and the three chairs. For dramatic effect, I move the chairs closer together and pull over another chair.

Julie and Joe sit down.

"What can I tell you, he called me." I offer as I sit down.

The waitress comes over.

"Can I get you three something?"

I see Caruso and Phillip already have a drink.

Julie jumps in, "I'll have a very dry vodka martini, 3 olives."

Impressive, "I'll have a Jack and water, on ice. He'll have a beer."

"Thanks, Dad."

We sit in silence until the waitress comes back with our drinks. I notice Bill walking into the bar. I'm glad I did not start my theory 101 class yet.

Forester walks over, he looks to be smiling.

Forester shakes everyone's hands, hugs Joe, and hugs me as well. I can't help giving him a pinch on the cheek to get a reaction. Forester smiles. Something is very wrong.

The waitress comes back for the next order. Bill looks up at her while sitting down, "I'll have a scotch on the rocks, single malt if possible."

The waitress leaves and returns in a minute.

Who will start, more importantly, who will finish? I prefer to do both.

"Thanks for coming. It's been a very hectic day. I couldn't believe how tired I was until we got here. Julie and Joe fell asleep as soon as I started driving….(I am babbling hoping Forester will jump in and tell us why he called me.) I could barely keep my eyes open while I was driving…."

Caruso cannot take another minute, "Bill please stop this nonsense before he starts explaining what his room looks like."

Forester laughs, "I wanted to see how long he would go on. Look, I got a call from Federal Marshal Copeland, he feels you guys are heading down a rabbit hole that you might not be able to get out of. Do you want to let me know what you have so far?"

Everyone at the table points to me knowing that I prefer taking the lead here and also knowing that I sometimes mix the facts up a bit.

"Do we need another round first; this might take a few minutes."

"Excuse me, can we get another round of drinks," blurts out Phillip just as I finish asking.

We all drink up as the waitress brings a fresh round, she also puts some baskets of chips, nuts, and assorted crap on the table.

Caruso waves at me to start.

Everyone settles in. I'm thinking of going Readers Digest version to throw everyone off.

Naaaaa.

"As you know, Joe applied to his wonderful school down here in the Sunshine State and got in, much to my chagrin. Nice reference letter by the way."

Joe cheers Bill with his glass.

"I digress, we were contacted by the college President, the late charred, Mr. Johnson. It seems some money has gone missing from his safe and a missing professor along with the supposed ten million dollars, though the amount is open for discussion. Thinking about the size of the safe I don't think ten million dollars would fit in it. You know they don't make thousand-dollar bills anymore. (I can hear people rolling their eyes.) When we arrived back at the president's office right before the blast, we noticed a gas odor and a gun's red laser scope pointing at the bookcase, we ran out just as the blast happened to render the dear Mr. Johnson dead or should I say, deader. He stopped breathing before the blast. This is when we got to meet Federal Marshal Copeland. Besides sweating a lot, we cannot figure him out yet. Oh yeah, our car got blown up, Caruso showed up – (I'm going faster and faster.) we got coffee, went back to campus, ran into the supposed missing professor, had a nice conversation with her in the massive library that Julie here has an access card to, we got pulled into a meeting with Julie's boss who's a nice guy and said we should stay on the case and our expenses would be handled, though probably not for this place. (Breath) We went to a cheap sleazy hotel where we met Mr. Stein who works for the NCAA in some capacity trying to get us to drop whatever we are doing which we don't know what we are doing. Caruso decided at that point to head home and Phillip found this lovely hotel for us which I seem to be paying for. Then things got interesting, we met Jilly Ricardo and his friend Mr. Farante and got to have lunch at a great golf club. I don't think we have enough cash to join it though I did get a putter for some reason. Julie and I came to the same conclusion; this Farante character is or was in the CIA. We then headed back to the campus when Joe felt he was being followed. We found Joe at a girls' volleyball game in the gym which I admit was a good choice to stay out in public. At least I thought it was a choice to be in, public you know, but during a break in the game, Julie and I are seated across from Joe who sees someone coming for him. We notice Jilly heading quickly for Joe and of course, I start to panic which I am getting incredibly good at, but Jilly surprises us and brings down one of two guys trying to get to Joe. Joe knocks the other guy down while Jilly takes care of the other guy. Security and the campus police rush in, and who should show up, Copeland. We give false information about knowing Jilly. He gets away. We catch up with him later as we blow off Copeland. Joe packs a bag and here we are."

The air has been sucked out of the room, Phillip gets up with glass in hand, and everyone follows his lead, except Forester, "That was amazing and pretty close." Forester looks up at Phillip, "Don't encourage him."

Forester is scaring me, without…. scaring me. We've been friends for a long time, and he is taking this pretty well. He doesn't like to be used, especially by me, and in some cases, that could ruin his career.

"OK, enough of the fun, how and why are you here?"

Phillip and the others sit down.

"With my retirement date approaching, I have been trying to figure out what I wanted to do. As you could imagine, my rank opens a lot of doors. Government consultant, private consultant, wall street or even a large international real estate construction firm or hang around the house, play golf and drive my wife nuts."

Forester takes a sip of his scotch. Dare I say it – cliché – the silence is deafening. Not really, it's just annoying.

"Let me guess, you want to be a private eye, well our little team is sucking the life out of our payroll and I don't think we could afford it…."

Caruso jumps in, "Executive in the NCAA!"

Forester raises his glass, "Close, VP of Operation for the NFL."

"Finally, good tickets," I exclaim.

Julie figures it's time to connect the dots, "Since I am figuring you have started in your new position, a Mr. Stein contacted you. The NCAA needs to keep the NFL apprised of something as big as this. Stein was contacted by the FBI about the missing money. Even though Henderson warned us about not getting in touch with you he called you."

"Yes, I've played a few rounds with Henderson over the years. Once he found out about my new upcoming position, he figured he was helping me protect your team and to make sure this case didn't screw up my new job."

"So, Uncle Bill, what's next?"

"Look, something like this does not stay out of the news for long. Throw a dead college President into this and the story runs around like a wildfire."

This has been one long day.

"Let me ask you something, do you even have a client?" Forester asks.

"I have a check that says so. This day could have been a lot worse unless you are the charbroiled Johnson. Too soon? Someone tried to blow us up at one point, they also tried to grab Joe right from the school. What is the official take from the NFL and NCAA?

Forester shakes him, "A robbery gone bad. Officially? Nothing was taken from the college."

I was about to go deeper into the Farante and Jilly story, but I'll hold this in my pocket.

Caruso decides to play cop, "You guys know this will all come out, plus you realize that the NFL is a private company that is notorious for covering things up and skirting the law. You have as much jurisdiction as Jamaica here. Julie at least is still with the FBI and I am still an NYC cop. Plus, if Jamaica is half right and this Farante character is with the CIA and is operating with or without their knowledge, this mess is just beginning. The CIA has no jurisdiction here in the states, so if they are working on something, we are looking at international criminals."

"I bet golf and chasing your wife around the house looks pretty good by now." I couldn't resist.

Forester takes another sip of his near-empty scotch, "Can I finish?" Forester reaches into his sport coat and pulls out an envelope. He puts it on the table with his hand firmly pressed down on it.

"You have a new client."

I try to pry the envelope from under his hand to no avail.

Phillip cannot help himself, "Oh this will work out fine."

"Jamaica, this needs to be handled with kit gloves."

"That's kid gloves, what does that mean?"

"I think Uncle Bill means cautiously."

"I can see where the brains in the family are located. We want information. We do not want anyone getting hurt."

"This coming from the NFL…. sorry." Sometimes I slip.

Forester gets up. "Please stay in touch; I really would like to stay in this job for a bit."

We all wait for Forester to walk out of the bar and into the hotel lobby.

"Look, I know the NCAA and the NFL keeps this payment stuff to student-athletes under a tight rein but something is not sitting right here. Everything I have ever read about in the past is that there is usually some shoe company that has paid off kids and their families to get a kid to sign with a certain college. I'm sure that boosters for a college lend a hand here too, therefore certain schools are always ranked high in the football standings year in and year out. But everything we are looking at here is pointing to an exceptionally large conspiracy. Ten million dollars in one location is a shit load of money and probably impossible to fit within the safe as we said earlier." I pause.

"Dad, if we are looking at gamblers could that explain the cash?"

Phillip shakes his head, "I haven't convinced its gamblers either. This isn't Chicago under Al Capone."

"Especially with these so-called legal gambling sites which make it so easy to gamble on any game at any time. There are still bookies out there handling hundreds of millions of dollars a year, but I agree with Phillip, ten million in one place seems a bit fishy," Caruso lets on.

"My office must know more than they are letting on, though I don't think they will offer much to me," Julie confesses.

"Unless we offer up a few leads to get them talking," I suggest.

"I don't know Dad, lying to the FBI, is that such a good idea?"

"I wouldn't consider it lying, misleading yes, but lying, not really."

"What will draw all the bad guys out of the shadows?" I ask.

Silence.

I can hear the wheels turning, they're working hard, and I can feel it. We are like a well-oiled machine. A team.

"I got nothing," Caruso admits.

"Me neither," I stare at Phillip, a mystery writer who has nothing. What the hell? I now look at Julie with that, WELL? look.

"I am drawing a blank myself," Julie shrugs.

"Come on Joe, I need one good thought here."

"We can let it out, probably to Copeland that we found a wire transfer that showed the money was gone before he called us to help him investigate. He used us as a ruse to keep people off his trail. Johnson is dead; he cannot get hurt anymore." Joe stares at us.

We're getting good at keeping silent. I will not get caught up in the thought that everyone is thinking hard, not again.

"This actually might work," Caruso offers and nods.

Phillip grabs his glass to make a point, "We need to add some back story here to keep everyone guessing. We don't want the heat to be placed on that Watson lady. We can say she was a patsy for Johnson."

"We can blame Johnson for everything," I admit this could work.

"Good job Joe."

"How do we construct this story?" Julie asks.

"Probably with another drink," Phillip suggests.

"I need to head home, all I ask is that you don't overdo it. I have seen Jamaica go off on one of these schemes before and it took two months to unravel it. We got so caught up chasing a bad cop one time that we used his innocent wife as a decoy. We busted the cop and forgot about the wife. The DA had her booked for embezzlement." Caruso remembers.

"Wait, if I remember, she had a good sense of humor about it. I saw her a year or two later, her life seemed pretty good." I charge.

"Jamaica, she sued the police department and ended up cashing in on a multimillion-dollar settlement," Caruso states emphatically.

"So, things worked out OK." I profess.

"Unbelievable, call me if you need a hand. Talk soon." Caruso walks out of the bar. So far two people have left the table, I'm seeing a pattern, and this check will be mine.

Phillip motions the waitress over for another round. I see a quizzical look on Joe's face. I turn around and see Caruso standing by the bar, trying to look inconspicuous. A familiar huge body is walking towards us, Jilly. I get up. Caruso starts heading back to the table expecting trouble. Caruso sees me stick out my hand to welcome Jilly, who shakes my hand gives me a friendly light slap on the check. Caruso gives a slight wave and turns and heads out.

"Hello, Julie, Joe, and??"

"This has to be Jilly," Phillip states.

"Phillip, Jilly, Jilly, Phillip." I offer up.

Jilly takes Caruso's seat. The waitress comes back with our drinks. "Can I get you anything, Jilly?" I politely offer.

"Coffee, thanks."

"Phillip…?" Jilly asks.

Phillip looks at me as if to say, do I tell him my name? I shrug as if to say why not.

"Meli."

"I thought so, I love your books. I'm impressed Mr. Biltmore, you have an interesting circle of friends. I cannot wait to meet the admiral."

I don't even want to ask. He probably knows my ex-wife. Maybe he can read minds. I need sleep.

"I need to ask; you seem to show up wherever we are. Do you spend all your day and night following us for Mr. Farante?" I ask with an attitude.

Jilly stirs the milk into his coffee, "Don't be silly, there's a GPS tracker in your car." Jilly takes a sip.

I cannot help but laugh. Julie does not look so happy. FBI agents rarely do.

"What can we help you with?' I have nothing to say to get him to talk.

Julie sees my uselessness. "Jilly, we don't understand what your participation in this case means."

"We like you Mr. Biltmore; you have had an interesting career. You do seem to solve cases well, though most are pretty mundane, but that last one, boy that was a real piece of work. Construction goons, the mob, city officials, that was some puzzle you put together." Jilly takes a sip of his coffee.

I hate the pause for dramatic effect. He's about to drop a bombshell. Another cliché is about to leak out all over the table. Phillip is about to ask a question, I kick him under the table and very slowly shake my head no. Joe notices my head shake, smirks, and takes a sip of his beer. Julie looks down into her drink and smiles before taking a sip.

95

Jilly takes a deep breath and sits back, "Remember in Superman III when Richard Pryor had the scheme to steal a penny from everyone's paycheck or something like that, well this is even better. Have you ever bought a football ticket online from a ticket broker or your favorite team website? Have you ever really looked at all the taxes and fees they add on, not really, I mean you might have gotten pissed about them, but no one questions them? No matter how sophisticated the teams and brokers are, they all figured someone else added these on, like each state. See there are a handful of companies that print the tickets for everyone. All the taxes for each state and fees that are paid go through a central system for each state…"

I close my eyes and chuckle, Jilly notices.

"You guessed it, someone hacked into a handful of systems, added a fee line to each ticket over the past fifteen years. Each team, broker, and state figured that the fee was put there by someone else. No one questioned it, ever," Jilly smirks.

We all just look at each other. There is no way to calculate this amount of money, but I need to try.

"How much are we talking about?" I ask baffled.

'We hear about five hundred million transactions a year from around the world. Think about it, sporting events, professional and college, concerts, Olympics,"

Phillip has a strange look on his face, "Wait a minute, over fifteen years that's about 7.5 billion transactions. They were probably not too greedy, very smart but not greedy. Let's say they tacked on 20 cents to stay under the radar, it's like 100 million dollars… A YEAR!"

"Very good Mr. Meli. Don't get me wrong, one hundred million is a nice sum, but once you get other people involved it gets carved up, and pretty soon it's good money, not great money."

Julie perks up, "Unless this is seed money used for other nefarious operations."

Jilly smiles broadly.

"CIA seed money," I suggest.

"Let me put it this way, we have been told through some good sources that over time, this money has grown to billions of dollars.."

"How the heck did…" Joe cannot control himself. I'm glad he asks.

"It seems these guys were pretty sharp, whenever they loaned out the money, they asked for collateral or a cut of the profits. Over fifteen years, do you know how many presidential administrations we went through and how many little countries changed hands? Nobody kept track or cared too. Everyone thinks cash is easy to come by."

Now I am lost, "how does this tie into our deep-fried Mr. Johnson?"

"It seems this little offshore organization has gone silent over the last two years. Nobody has been able to get a cent out of them. The spigot has dried up. The company started chasing down the accounts and found them sitting in an account in Cuba. Nothing moved in and out for months."

"Let me guess, and then ten million got wired to Mr. Johnson." I surmise.

"Maybe more." Jilly finishes his coffee.

"So, Johnson hired us under the premise that this money was college football money? He figured if he told the truth, we wouldn't get involved." I throw out.

Phillip shakes his head as if something is not sitting right, he tightens his lips which I have known to mean he has some thoughts but will keep them himself until Jilly leaves.

Jilly stands up, "I gotta run, it's been an interestingly long day. I will stay in touch, be careful."

Jilly pats me on the back as he walks out of the bar. I get up and walk over to the bar to close out the tab. I pay the bartender and walk back to the table.

"Do you want to sit on your theory or give us your thoughts upstairs?" I ask Phillip.

Julie, Joe, and Phillip get up at the same time, "I would rather give this some thought tonight and have it rattle around in that brain of yours until morning."

We walk in silence to the elevator, hit the button, and wait. I cannot help but think there are too many parts to this case that don't make sense. We have two clients who paid in advance which is not normal which makes me think something is fishy. The elevator opens, we hit our floor. More silence. The door opens and we stumble out, we're all exhausted. We walk down the hallway to our door.

Chapter 22

Glass Break Sensor

I take out the key and swipe the electronic lock. I hold the door for the group to enter.

"Stop."

"What's wrong Jamaica?" Phillip asks.

"Don't touch anything" I say as I raise my hands to stop everyone in their tracks.

"Dad, why is your luggage on the bed?"

"What…" Julie mutters.

"Dad never puts his luggage on the bed, he thinks it's a disgusting thing to do."

"Mine is still on the floor," Julie states.

"I took some things out using the luggage stand and put it back on the floor."

Phillip slowly walks over to the bed, all I can think about is 'oh shit, and we are going to blow up a Ritz. This will not look good on our resume.' He bends down slowly with his head looking sideways at the luggage. It hits me, I lunge for Phillip and push him towards the wall as a bullet crashes through the window and hits me spinning me around onto the floor.

"Dad!!"

"Stay there. I'm ok," as I grasp my arm. The bullet grazed me and lodged into the bathroom shower wall.

Julie grabs a towel and kneels beside me to check out my arm. She pulls me away from the line of fire. Phillip crawls away from the bed as well, and back into the living area of the room. I get to my feet and slowly make my way to a window in the other room to look in the vicinity of where the shot could have come from. Through the dark, I can see a parking lot but it's far away. We are talking expert shooters. Julie grabs me away from the window. She opens my shirt to see the damage from the bullet. It's a deep graze, but it will heal. No bullet hole. Lots of blood though, we'll need more towels.

"Well, we now know we are on the right track. What track that is I'm not sure," Phillip smirks. He walks over to the minibar and grabs out a little Johnny Walker Black bottle, cracks the top foil seal, and hands it to me.

I look up at him, "Thanks, but can I have a glass."

Everyone takes a seat, on the floor.

"Now tell us about that theory of yours Phillip."

"Is now a good time for this? One of us could have been killed here."

"I am not sure any of us are getting much sleep right now. So, after what just happened does your theory still hold water?"

"Dad, I want to stay here tonight, I can sleep on the sofa."

I try not to look at Julie, but she jumps in, "I think that's a good idea, Joe."

I glare at Phillip.

"Don't look at me, I am going to my room," Phillip states.

So far no one is knocking on our door since the window was shot out.

"Ok, do we think that there is a connection between the NCAA, NFL, and a CIA shell company which seems to be sitting on a couple of hundred million dollars? Could Johnson have been skimming money from this CIA slush fund to replace a few million dollars that was supposed to be used to pay off these college athletes? Maybe he is the common denominator?"

"Let's say he is working both sides of this to what end? We have been paid money from a supposed CIA agent and the NFL, again, to what end?" I question.

"The CIA wants to get hold of what they think is their money and the NFL is just trying to protect their brand." Julie states.

"What about the gambling end of this and who wants you, dead Dad?"

I take a large sip of my scotch, look down at my arm, "Why take a shot at me now? Who wins by stopping us??"

"Well, we know Forester has nothing to do with this unless he is being used. We know nothing about Jilly, do we? I think it's time I ask Henderson some questions," Julie suggests.

"In the morning," I state. "I need sleep. Phillip, can you walk Joe to his room to get his stuff?"

"Sure."

"Stay away from the windows."

Joe and Phillip head out of the room. Julie helps me up, "You ok?

"Yeah, we'll need to bring Caruso up to speed tomorrow. Thanks for being Ok with Joe staying here."

Julie kisses me, "I wouldn't have had it any other way. Safety in numbers."

"Or easier to hit someone with the next shot."

Finally, the day comes to an end. Sleep could not be more welcome right now. The arm stings but I have had worse. We've all finished our nighttime routines. I look at Julie and Joe and I admire the grit of this group. We are a tough group. I try to relax and get the day out of my mind so I am not up all night. I look over and Joe and Julie seem to be asleep already. I chuckle to myself — some tough group — all three of us sleeping on the floor.

Chapter 23

Square One

I'm the first one up and out. I close the living area door to the bedroom so I can grab some clothes and shower. I take a sneak peek from the side of the window to check out the weather outside. After a quick shower, and shave, I dress and slowly make my way past Joe and Julie who are sprawled out on the floor and out the door of the suite. Reaching for my phone from my pocket I quickly head for the elevator bank. I text Caruso as to what happened last night. I hit send and it seems a second later the phone rings.

"We're ok. My arm is a bit sore from the graze. No, why would you say that? We slept in the beds, why would we sleep on the floor? Let me grab some coffee and we will call you later and bring you up to speed on what our day is like."

I hit the elevator button to head down to the lobby. I ride alone in the elevator. The door opens, I see Phillip walking towards me with his coffee.

"How's the arm?"

"It's ok. How's the coffee?"

"Fine, you guys sleep on the floor?"

"Why would you say that?" I don't wait for an answer, I head for the coffee bar. What a silly name for a coffee shop. I wait in line and order three coffees and three muffins. As I sign my name and room number to the check, I feel a meaty hand on my arm.

Jilly. I grab my coffees and muffins and turn away from the counter. Standing in the lobby is Mr. Farante.

"I think we need to talk, JB." Jilly looks from me to Farante.

JB, I am starting not to like this guy, "I'd like to bring the coffee to my co-workers."

"I think it can wait." Jilly leads me gently through the lobby and outside into the marvelous warm sunshine. Farante doesn't acknowledge me, he just follows Jilly and me out the overly large glass sliding doors.

Farante walks over, grabs the three coffees, hands me one, one to Jilly and one for himself, "Let's walk and talk."

Jilly has worry lines across his face. Last night he was in control. I'm not sure if Farante has this effect on him or not. At the end of the long walkway leading from the front door of the hotel to the parking lot, is a white van with blackened windows. I cannot help feeling that van is for me.

We get closer to the van but we have yet to start talking. This is not a good sign. Farante looks at Jilly, "Let's walk around the back, there have to be some tables or something to sit at."

The words are barely out of his mouth as the van doors slam open and three guys jump out. We freeze in our tracks, pool cleaners. Damn it. I try and look cool by taking a sip of my coffee and nod to the three workers.

I hear Jilly giggle, yup, giggle.

Farante is up ahead and walking towards a gazebo off the sidewalk around the side of the hotel. Jilly and I seem both a bit more at ease. The three of us enter the gazebo and take a seat. I open the bag of muffins and offer the bag to Farante and Jilly who both decline.

"I know Jilly gave you an overview of what we think is going on with the missing money. We're not interested in this NCAA, NFL connection. We have no authority here to investigate legally. I am only interested in getting back the money that is missing. I know it might not seem like it, but this money does a lot of good things around the world."

I'm not buying this.

"There is a connection in Cuba that we'll chase down. We'll let you know. You work your end of things and we'll follow up with you in a few days."

I reach up to my arm because I feel something wet dripping down my arm. Blood.

"What the hell happened to you?" Farante inquires.

"I cut myself shaving," As the words leave my mouth Farante's shoulder explodes all over me and Jilly.

Jilly pulls all three to the ground. I search for the location of the shooter. Nothing. I press against the hole in Farante's shoulder. Jilly takes out a phone and calls for help. A young man on the sidewalk runs for the front door of the hotel.

"Jilly, go get me a few towels, I need to keep the pressure on this."

Jilly gets up and runs towards the hotel, he passes Joe and Julie who have come running out. I'm guessing the guy who ran into the hotel lost his cool and they came running. Joe and Julie get to me at the same time.

"What the hell happened?" Julie screams at me.

I turn as I keep pressure with my hand, "We were chatting when this shot rang out."

Farante tries to get up, I push him back down. Jilly comes puffing back with a few towels. He hands me one. A crowd has gathered. I hear the sirens coming up the long drive. People point them towards us. The ambulance comes to a halt and two EMT's rush out. They take over from me. I need another shower.

The EMTs slowly help Farante up and take him into the back of the ambulance. People are whispering as the manager of the hotel approaches. Jilly intercepts him from reaching me. He guides him back towards the hotel. Julie, Joe, and I watch as the crowd disperses, and the ambulance pulls away with the wounded Farante. Jilly comes out of the hotel and heads towards us. I didn't realize the blood splatter got him as well. His shirt is a mess.

I turn to Joe, "Please go in the gift shop and get a golf shirt for Jilly, extra-large."

Joe does not answer me, he walks away and past Jilly who stops for a second and says something to Joe.

Julie and I head to him, I need to shower and grab another cup of coffee. I can't help but wonder where Phillip is. The sun is getting warmer but I have a feeling we're not going to have time to enjoy it.

We meet up with Jilly.

"That is a good kid you have; you should have let him go to college without the pressure of having him join you in this crazy business."

"Let's get inside and away from prying eyes."

Julie walks ahead of us, "I'll get coffee and meet you in the room."

"Ok," I am sure she wants to make a call.

Jilly and I walk with a purpose into the hotel. I finally notice Phillip, the hotel manager and what I imagine to be a detective, chatting in the coffee bar. Again, it's a silly name.

Jilly and I make our way into the elevator without either of them noticing us. I hit our floor button and as usual, we ride up in silence.

Chapter 24

Make Your Bed and Lie In It

"One thing is bothering me."

Jilly makes his way to a chair, "One thing?"

"Ok, everything is bothering me." I pick through my bag to get a clean shirt and pants.

Julie walks into the room with three coffees, followed by Joe with a shirt for Jilly in a hotel bag. Joe hands it to Jilly.

"Thanks, kid."

"It was my dad's idea. Walking around with blood-stained clothes can turn off a lot of people."

"It can be a deterrent too," Jilly states as he heads to the bathroom to switch shirts.

I take the coffee from Julie, "How'd the call go?"

"I'll tell you later, please go shower and take off those clothes."

Jilly walks out of the bathroom with a fresh shirt on. I walk past him with my clothes in hand and coffee in the other. I need these few minutes to unravel my thoughts. I close the bathroom door and run the shower, the hot water feels great. I cannot help putting my finger in the bullet hole in the shower wall. Staring at the wall, and it hits me, I scrub fast and shut the water off. My arm is still sore. I towel off quickly and dress. I walk out all dressed and smelling clean, I grab a plastic laundry bag from the bedroom closet for my blood-stained clothes. I walk back into the living room to complete silence.

"Something is bothering me, Jilly. You don't seem very bothered by your boss getting shot. Let me show you something." I motion for Jilly to step into the bedroom.

Jilly gets up.

From my side of the bed, I point to broken glass and then to the bullet hole in the shower wall. Jilly doesn't say anything. I walk back into the living room. There is a knock on the door. Jilly stops and stays in the bedroom. Julie looks through the peephole and opens the door. Phillip.

Jilly continues walking into the living area.

I give a slight side-to-side shake of my head and mouth – NO to Phillip.

"You were saying JB?" Jilly sits back down.

"Farante is not your boss and you two are not working for the same company, correct?"

"I'm guessing no one got hurt from the errant shot last night. Well except for your arm, which I am sure will heal. I think you assumed that I work for Farante. I don't believe we ever said it. Let me ask you a question, do you think that shot was meant for Farante?"

I stare at Jilly not offering up anything.

"I figured it was for me since someone missed last night or you. We are looking at a desperate killer." Jilly states.

"And a bad shot," chimes in Phillip. We all stare at him. "Just saying, it seems strange doesn't it?"

"Maybe someone is trying to scare us off Dad."

"Who did you call Ms. Waters?"

Julie looks at Jilly. She stays silent.

"Phillip, what went on downstairs?"

Phillip looks at me and raises his eyebrows.

"It doesn't matter Phillip; Jilly seems to find out everything that's going on anyway."

"The cops were called off immediately from swarming the place. The hotel manager was taken care of and his staff was warned not to spread any stories."

"That never stops anyone talking. Dad, I think we need a plan or we need to somehow drop this case."

Jilly looks up at me, "You have our money and a nice check from your admiral friend. You can give it all back or you can help."

"I need to know who I am helping." I know I would like to ask him how he keeps showing up so fast but I'd rather work that out myself and use it against him later.

"Ok, your son is probably right; if someone wanted to shoot you, they would have been able to do it unless they are a really bad shot. Most guys who get hired to take someone out usually don't miss twice. So, let's go with the idea that it is a warning. Farante works for the money people. They are trying to get their ten million back but most importantly they need to know if more money has been disappearing. Yes, I work for a certain government agency and you are right we have no jurisdiction here at all. We have a big interest in the money staying in hands that we can trust. We still have not figured out Johnson's role in all this. We haven't made any connections between him and the money people. His death is a real mystery so far. By calling you into this the profile of this case has gotten to such a high point that it makes it very delicate to dispose of." Jilly takes a large swig of his coffee. He sucked the air out of the room.

Jilly gets up and heads for the door, "Be careful, there is still a shooter out there."

There is nothing to say at this point. Jilly walks out.

I turn to Julie, "I'm guessing that the gentleman with the hotel manager was FBI?"

"He was."

"What are you thinking Dad?"

"What if those shots were a message to steer clear and what if those shots were arranged by Jilly?"

I see the shock in everyone's face except Julie, "You don't seem too surprised by my statement."

"I was thinking the same thing, I think Jilly got spooked when I didn't answer him when he asked who I called. Henderson says no one has any idea who he is."

"Wouldn't that just mean he is a good spy?" Phillip hopes.

Julie gets up and throws out her empty cup, "Only in a good book Phillip, like yours."

Phillip smiles.

I have no idea where to go from here. I walk into the bathroom and the shower. I stick my finger in the bullet hole. I look out the window at the parking garage across the way. The lot is higher than the building explaining where the shooter shot from. "Julie, Phillip, come in here."

Julie and Phillip are both staring at me with my finger in the bullet hole, "I think this is a 22, what do you two think?"

Julie steps into the shower, I pull my finger out, she looks closer, "I agree."

"Ok, back into the living room."

Julie and Phillip walk back into the living area, I follow with the bag of bloody clothes in my hand. I pull out my shirt.

"I was standing a foot or two away from Farante when he got shot."

Phillip chuckles, "That's a lot of blood for a 22."

"The hole in his shoulder was made by a large caliber bullet. There is no way a shooter would bring two different guns with him." I offer.

"Nor would he wait through the night on the off chance that you would be walking around the grounds in the morning, especially not knowing if the shot last night hit its mark," Joe says.

"Let's say last night was meant for you, and today we have a different shooter looking to take out either Farante or Jilly," surmises Julie.

"I don't feel so safe staying around this hotel waiting for a shooter who is good at his job. I think we call Caruso and get his thoughts. Let's put some clothes in a small bag and stay checked in here. It might keep someone guessing as to what we are up to." Phillip doesn't wait for our answer, he walks out of his room.

"Ok, I guess we have a plan." Joe and Julie are not waiting for me, they have started to throw some clothes and essentials into one bag. I pick through my bag for a few clean things and grab my overnight bag. My phone rings, Phillip.

"OK, see you downstairs."

I grab my bloody clothes, Julie, Joe, and I head out the door and towards the elevator. We hit the down button nervously waiting for the elevator to open. As if on cue, the elevator dings signaling the arrival. On instinct, the three of us step aside as the elevator doors open revealing an empty cab. A bunch of chickens.

We get in, "You do have my stuff, right?"

Julie looks at me, "A lot of good they did us."

"It just feels good to have them close by."

Joe smiles and stands closer to Julie.

The elevator opens and we head towards Phillip who is chatting with the manager. He points to us, "We are all keeping our rooms for the next few days, and we'll be back later."

"We're going to visit friends and enjoy the weather. Oh, by the way, there's a small crack in our bedroom window. I'm sure that's not good for the air conditioning," I hand the manager the bag with my bloody clothes, "Can I get this laundered? They have some stains that might be tough to get out."

"Certainly, Mr. Biltmore." I reach into my pocket for a tip. The manager puts up his hand, "That will not be necessary, your friend this morning was very generous to us."

"Ok then, see you later."

Joe and Julie are already standing outside. Phillip and I join them, I hand the valet my ticket and he runs to get my car.

I grab my phone and dial Caruso, "Hey what's up? ……. At the airport? Is everything OK?………………
Oh, sorry to hear that. We were going to catch up with you, spend the day, and enjoy the sun, you know a little

relaxing time……. What, no, we are doing great ……
……… OK, twice, they missed both times ………..
Great see you in 30 minutes …………. A great hiding
place for a key."

The kid brings my car, we pile in. We drive down
the long driveway and out of the hotel entrance.

"Sarah is heading back to New York, a friend of hers
is sick. We'll meet Caruso at his house."

"The key is under the entrance mat?" Phillip guesses
correctly.

Julie's phone goes off, she listens for a few seconds,
"OK, got it, Surf Beach."

"Henderson wants us to pull into the beach up on
the right, Surf Beach, pull to the far right of the parking
lot. A white van." Julie commands.

I drive as instructed, "Of course it's a white van, I'm
sure they're wearing those blue windbreakers with the
large letters on the back, ha."

"Have they been waiting on the slim chance we
would be leaving now or are we being watched?" Joe asks.

I look at Julie.

"Don't look at me."

"Is your phone company issued?" I stare at Julie.

"It is but…."

"This is not good. We don't know who we can
trust." Phillip misspeaks.

Julie turns around with a death stare.

Philip jumps knowing his mistake, "I meant Henderson, and I would never think that about you."

I am letting him dig himself in deeper. I tap Julie on
the arm and point as I pull to the nondescript, but obvious FBI white van.

"You two stay here. Hold my bag." I hand to no one particular in the back seat.

Joe takes it from me, "Not me." He hands it to Phillip.

Julie and I get out of the car, the van's sliding door opens, and Henderson gets out and slides the door shut. I was hoping to see if we had company in the van. Henderson does not seem like the driving a white van type. So, for now, I will figure there is at least one other agent in there. I don't like this. I'll let Julie do most of the talking. He must know everything since there was an agent in the lobby quickly this morning.

"Are you both ok? My agent told me what happened. How the hell did you get involved with Farante and Jilly?"

Julie looks at me, I put out my hand as if to go ahead.

"They contacted us." She confesses.

` "Copeland, it has to be him. I asked you nicely to not involve your admiral friend." Julie and I are silent. Henderson looks back and forth at us. "He called you, didn't he? I was afraid of that. I didn't think his new position with the NFL started yet. Damn, another bunch of knuckleheads getting involved. Talk about an organization sitting on a pedestal."

I cannot keep silent anymore, it's not in me, "Not a football fan?"

"I love football, I am not a fan of their business practices. Just a personal grudge, I guess. Never mind. Have you heard from the guy from NCAA again?"

"Nothing sir,"

"Ok, I will give you what we got as long as you do the same."

"Sure." Is my sarcastic response.

"Very convincing Mr. Biltmore, Ok, we don't think Farante is who he says he is. We do think Jilly is CIA, hopefully, he is still with them. Whenever I have a case that smells of CIA involvement, they always deny the person I ask them about. We all know they're not allowed to operate within the United States, so when I asked my CIA contact, he had that 'Oh Shit' look on his face."

"That was it, just a hunch?" I ask.

` "I'd rather not say what he said."

"Sir let us in on it. Jamaica has a way of working through these things. His instincts are surprisingly good…. for a PI."

I don't think she would use that word, surprisingly. I throw a few eye darts at Julie and I will remember to bring that up with her later. Who am I kidding, I won't bring that up.

Henderson looks at me, takes a deep breath, "You know the song, You Don't Tug On Superman's Cape, You Don't Spit in The Wind, You Don't Pull the Mask Off the Long Ranger and you don't mess around with…"

"Jilly…?" I guess.

"That's it in a nutshell," Henderson says apologetically.

"He said that?" I asked hoping it was true, I always wanted to use that line.

"He did. These guys are a bit loopy. Look, wherever you are headed you need to figure someone is watching. I have a limited amount of resources working on this case. If either of you gets shot, I am sure we can free up a few more agents."

Julie and I both look at him incredulously. (I am not sure what that looks like.)

"Kidding."

I was about to show him the grazed arm but the last thing we want is to be followed around all day. Though I think he is doing it anyway we don't have to let on we know. Understand?

"I will call you later sir,"

"Let me ask you a question, we have a case involving possibly the CIA, the NCAA, the NFL, and some very large overseas bank accounts, and let us not forget, a deep-fried president of a major college and the FBI is holding back resources?"

"Exactly Mr. Biltmore, Washington DC got involved pretty early which makes me think this case is well above all our pay grade. This is why I can feed information to you, I cannot chase this down." Henderson doesn't look back; he slides open the van's door and steps in.

I look at Julie. "Let's head to Caruso's and run this down." Julie gets in the car first, I put my hand on the car's handle, stop in my tracks and pull away from the door. I take out my phone and dial. I walk away from the car. All eyes are on me.

"Hey, I need to talk with Admiral Forester, not NFL Forester, do you think you can pull that off? .... Good. Any chance you can meet at Caruso's house?...... We will be there most of the day, there are things I need to bring up, and hoping Navy Intelligence can help. If not, maybe you can get us some football tickets....... What?.. He's got a boat in his backyard?.......... No, we are not going out, I have had enough of that on the last case......I agree Pensions are great. Yes, you told me so thirty years ago. You and Caruso nailed it. .... See you later." I hit the end and get in the car mumbling to myself about the lecture from Forester.

Joe, Phillip, and Julie are staring at me waiting for me to explain. I start driving.

"Dad?"

"I called Bill; we need his help."

Phillip sits back rejected, "You mean NFL Forester?"

"No, I told him we need Admiral Forester today, he agreed."

"Did you know Caruso lives on the water and he has a boat in his backyard?"

Phillip chuckles, "Everyone down here lives on the water, kind of silly not to."

We ride in silence until "I keep thinking that we have forgotten about Johnson." Joe throws out there.

"He has a point," Julie agrees.

I would like to attend the funeral. Maybe we can piece some things together. I am thinking that I might not be the right person to go. We will send Caruso!

"I have an idea; I think we should attend the funeral for Johnson. I know, people will recognize us, at least Miss Lee will. That is why I thought of sending...."

"Caruso!" Julie blurts out.

"Exactly." I am so proud she is thinking like me. Not sure how helpful that is but we are on the same page.

We head down to Caruso's house on the coast. Everyone settles in for the ride. I reach for the phone and Julie slaps my hand. I stare at her.

"If you are going to talk on the phone I can drive and you can talk all day," Julie states emphatically.

"Can't we hook this thing up to the car?"

Julie takes the phone, hits buttons all over the place on the radio and my phone, and before I know it she is done, kids today. "Who would you like to talk to?"

I need to be careful how I ask her to do this… "Can you dial Copeland?"

I see everyone perk up, "What are you up to?" asks Phillip.

My thought process is interrupted by Copeland screaming at me over the car's speakers. "What's up Biltmore?"

"I have a thought; how can we inquire with the schools accounting department about the transaction between The NCAA and the school after their bowl game win. I would like to know how the payment is made."

"Interesting thought. Give me a few hours, I'll call you back. Where are you?"

"We are taking a ride down the coast. We can use a break." I offer up. "Oh, I think a bookkeeper might offer more help than the accounting boss."

"Good thought, I will call you back." The phone goes dead.

"What are you thinking Dad?"

"Since Johnson is dead, I am thinking everyone would want to protect themselves and we just might have someone offering up some information that we could use."

"Or everyone could have headed for the hills," Phillip states sarcastically.

The phone rings and Julie hit the green button, "Hello?"

"This is Pamela Watson, can I speak with Mr. Biltmore."

I frown, "Go ahead Ms. Watson, I am on speaker-phone in the car."

"Can I speak freely, Mr. Biltmore?"

"Yes."

"My dad would like to speak with you. (Pause, Pamela's dad gets on the call) Mr. Biltmore, How is the case going. Do you have any leads to help solve this case?"

"I understand you are an ex-policeman, from where?"

"Miami."

"We're hitting a few dead ends. We don't have a client anymore. So, we are laying low for a while."

"What about everyone else who is investigating this case? The feds, the NCAA, and the local police have they any leads?"

I can't help but look at Julie and Phillip in the back seat with a frown on. "As far as I know they are struggling. They think that whoever took the money is gone. It looks like the school is out a few million dollars from that bowl game. It was probably a low-level robbery who targeted Johnson for the money in his safe."

"Thank you, Mr. Biltmore."

"Can I speak to your daughter?"

Pam comes back on the phone, "Yes Mr. Biltmore?"

"Pam, do you know when the funeral is for Mr. Johnson?"

"Tomorrow night, I'd like to go but I'm still a bit worried. It's right near the campus, there is a funeral parlor on the corner by the entrance."

"Thank you, if we hear anything we'll let you know." I motion Julie to hit the end.

"Anyone find that conversation with her dad a bit strange?"

"He never once talked about the threat to his daughter." Julie states.

"That was weird, I don't get it. OK, we need to get Caruso to agree to head to the funeral parlor tomorrow and snoop around."

"Dad, my phone says we need to turn in here. Davenport Dr, 3801."

I make my way off the highway and onto Caruso's block. There is a gate splitting the drive-in and drive-out but no gates. I guess they don't pay enough for gates. All the houses are in perfect shape, they all look alike though. The landscaping around the property is perfect. Hard not to like a place like this. I scan the numbered signs on the lawns for Caruso's address. I see a familiar Jeep in the driveway. Forester. I forgot about him coming here. I'm not sure I'm ready for this conversation. I thought I had this worked out in my head but not any longer. I need to put out of my thoughts the strange conversation I had with Mr. Watson. We pull into the driveway and pile out of the car. I take a deep breath, I love the salt air coming off the water. Joe rings the bell.

Loudly – "It's open."

Joe opens the door, we all walk in.

CHAPTER 25

CHUM

The house is a typical Florida house. Tile floors, large glass doors open to a small patio where Caruso and Forster are enjoying a beer. I don't look at the rest of the house when I spot the dock fifty feet from the patio doors. A wonderful 20-foot fishing boat bobs up and down in the slow surf. This is a fabulous space.

"Come in, there's cold beer in the frig in the kitchen." Caruso offers.

Phillip plays host and grabs six cold beers. Joe gives him a hand. Caruso gets up and grabs a chair from the side of the house. I can't help but head to the dock. Caruso follows me.

"This is great. Are you thinking of buying it?" I ask Caruso.

"I think so if not this one then another one in the neighborhood. All the houses are around the same size and we know a few guys from New York that live here. Sarah feels comfortable. The airport is close so trips back to New York will be easy. How does this compare where you are settling?"

Julie has walked over to look at the water.

"It's kind of the same. There is a nice town within walking distance. The water is all the same. Perfect."

"What have you got that you dragged Forester here?"

"Let's go chat, I have a favor to ask."

"This can't be good; he is being nice," Caruso says to Julie.

"Wait for it." Julie laughs.

We walk back to the patio table.

"Look, we know we have a few wild cards here like Farante, Jilly, the dead Johnson, and the entire football world. Bill, this is really off the record, we are talking with the Admiral, not the NFL. Jilly dropped a bombshell on us, and we think the FBI might know something about this. It seems there has been this scheme going on for at least fifteen years. There's a ticket scam that has kicked off over a billion dollars in cash."

I stare at Caruso and Forester who seem to have swallowed their beer cans.

"Do you believe this guy?" Asks Caruso to no one in particular.

"It is so farfetched it's hard not to, I am not sure Phillip here could come up with a story like this." My phone goes off on cue. I reach in my pocket, it's Copeland.

"Go ahead. Yes, it's me. (Listening) (Chuckling slightly to myself.) No, it was a hunch. Thanks."

Julie looks at me, "Copeland?"

I shake my head incredulously if that is possible.

"Dad?"

I know that Caruso and Forster have no idea what this is all about, I figured I would explain first. "I asked Copeland to investigate if anyone in the school's accounting department could tell him about how the football bowl money was received by the school and how it was deposited. I asked him to stick with a low-level bookkeeper if possible since they would normally tell the truth while a boss might want to cover things up, especially if it's missing."

"What did he find out?" asks Joe.

"It got wired in seven days after the game, it's all there and accounted for."

Everyone takes a sip at once.

"So that means Johnson was lying and maybe just maybe Jilly might have something with his tall tale." Phillip laughs to himself and walks towards the water.

"What was the favor you were going to ask me for?" Caruso questions.

"Johnson's funeral is tomorrow, I can't go, and no one has seen you I figured you won't attract attention."

"What will I be looking for?"

"I don't know. Use your cop instincts. We got a call while coming down here from the missing professor I spoke about yesterday, Pamela Watson. Her dad wanted to talk to us. He asked a lot of questions about the case and if we have any leads. But he never asked if his daughter was in any further danger."

"What the hell, I will go."

Forester gets up to leave, "Why am I here?"

Julie looks at me, she knows I am scrambling now so she jumps in. "Bill, is it possible to do a deep dive background on this Jilly Riccardo character? What we have so far is that he is CIA and this Farante guy is a money guy, maybe he sets up these large deals with people that normally do not do business with banks."

Forester looks at Julie, "Sure, let me make a call." Forester heads into the house for some private time.

I shake my head. If I would have asked, it would have taken an hour to get the same results that Julie got in 5 minutes. I turn to Caruso. "Any food?"

"We'll order in, anyone in for a quick trip on the water?"

Everyone nods in agreement. "Let's wait for Bill to get back out here then we'll order food and head out for a spin."

Forester returns rather quickly from inside the house. He looks at me, "It seems your Jilly was in the CIA and has been dismissed, to put it nicely, on a mental issue."

"Was this from Stevenson?" I ask Forester.

"You know Director Stevenson?" Julie asks impressed.

"We went to the academy together. Yes, I called him. He made a call while I was on hold."

I shake my head.

"What, you do not believe him?" Forester stares at me.

"Remember in the 'In-Laws' when Alan Arkin calls the CIA to ask about Peter Faulk and they tell him he was kicked out for a – are you ready for this – a MENTAL."

"Are you trying to compare this to a movie?"

"A great movie, but that is not the point." OK, I made a poor inference. "The head of the CIA is not going to tell us if one of their spies is working in the States.

Even if Jilly has gone rogue. Stevenson doesn't want a shit storm falling on him. As we all know the CIA is not allowed to operate within the States."

"That's a good point, now what do you need from me?" Forester asks.

Shaking my head dejected, "I'm not sure. I think more things will come to light after the funeral."

"Wake." Phillip throws out there, he looks at all of us, "It's a wake, the funeral is the service and the burial. Everyone makes that mistake."

"Whatever." I notice Julie walking away from the group grabbing her phone. She talks for a minute and comes back. "The WAKE is at 2 pm tomorrow."

"Ok, we have time. I think we lay low for the day and hopefully, nobody will take a shot at us while we hang out…." I let that hang in the air as I go for another beer.

"Really Dad?"

"What is my cover and the reason I'm at the wake?" Caruso asks.

I walk back outside with an arm full of beer and place them on the table.

"There will be so many people there I think any cover works. This was the president of a large school." Julie states.

"I think we get there a bit early and watch the people coming and going so we give Caruso some history of the people arriving."

"Sounds like a plan, lets order some food and go for a ride in the boat." Caruso offers.

"What food joints are good around here?" Joe asks.

"You all like lobster rolls?"

We all look at each other and nod.

"I need to head home, call me after the wake." Forester gets up and walks out of the yard.

"Ok, I'll order five lobster rolls and fries. I will go pick them up, No one will take a shot at me, and I am not famous like you guys."

Caruso walks inside and I can see him on the phone in his kitchen. Caruso calls out for the kitchen, "I'll be back in twenty."

I walk to the boat and jump on. Julie trails and I give her a hand getting on. I sit in the captain's seat with a beer in my hand. I finally feel relaxed. Julie stands next to me with her hand on my shoulder.

"What are you thinking?"

"I feel relaxed. This feels good. I think I can get used to being down here. Working is another issue. What about you? Can you work down here, I mean back at the bureau?"

"With your connections, I could pick my office. That's something that never happens in my line of work. I like the job; the pay is good and the benefits are great."

Phillip and Joe step over the bulkhead and into the boat. Phillip grabs a cooler from the back of the boat and heads back into the house. I am guessing to fill it up.

"Is everything ok Dad?"

"Perfect Joe, I think I can get used to being down here. What about you?"

"I can, I think we have the perfect place, I can hopefully stay in school without getting shot and you can be close by. It would be nice to see you both when I want."

I see Julie well up, she walks over to Joe and hugs him.

127

We better not get killed or this good feeling will stop.

Phillip comes back to the boat and hands the cooler to Joe who places it in the back of the boat. Julie looks at me, "I'm going to go to the bathroom before we go, I don't see one on the boas and if I did, I'm not sure I want to use it." Julie steps off the boat and heads for the house to use the bathroom.

"I think I'll go before we head out too." I also step off the boat and head for the house. I walk up the path and into the house. I catch Julie coming out of the bathroom.

"You OK?"

Julie looks at me and hugs me, "I know the first case was a bit dangerous, but this one seems to have taken an ugly turn. In my line of work, we have the good guys and the bad guys. I'm so unsure of what's in front of us. Are you worried?"

"I was, at the end of the day its pieces that need to fit into the puzzle. I think we are close. I do."

Caruso walks in right at that moment. His arms are full. I kiss Julie and walk over to help Caruso.

Caruso looks at us, "You guys OK?"

Julie straightens up, "We are, this case has me worried a bit, it's a bit stressful, I think the bad guys are different than what we have seen before, even in my career. These people seem over the top to achieve their end goal."

Caruso hands me the bag, grabs some napkins from the kitchen counter, and starts walking out to the boat. He stops and turns to Julie.

"Has he ever told you about meeting a movie star, a TV star, and a Beatle?" Caruso leaves the statement in midair.

"A Beatle??" Julie screams at Caruso. She looks at me.

I pull Julie out the door while holding the dinner, "Shall I pull the slider shut?"

Caruso looks back at me, "Oh yeah, please."

"Are you going to tell me the story?"

I lead Julie back to the boat, "Let's get on the boat, Joe has never heard this story, I am not sure Phillip has either."

I help Julie onto the boat. Caruso is priming the engine and getting us hoisted off. We all settle into our seats. Caruso heads the boat out of the canal and into the bay. The water is very calm, and the sun is going to be setting within a few hours. Caruso turns to us, "Any place particular or shall I find a nice calm place to eat and we can drive around after."

"Sounds good to me." chimes in Joe.

"Good to me." Phillip agrees.

Caruso does not wait for me to answer, he pulls into a secluded part of the bay facing west so we can enjoy the warm sun as we eat. Caruso slows down and cuts the engine then looks at me. Without saying anything I get up and walk to the front of the boat and wait for him to signal me to throw the anchor. Caruso waves to me, and I throw the anchor off. Caruso throws the engine in reverse to tighten the anchor and he gives me a thumbs-up, I walk around back.

Phillip is already opening the bag and handing out the lobster rolls. Julie opens the cooler and hands beers to everyone. Julie cannot wait for another second, she turns to Phillip, "Have you ever heard of these two guys meeting one of the Beatles?"

Phillip looks back and forth between Caruso and me with his mouth open.

"Dad, you met a Beatle and never said anything?"

I look at Caruso, "I kind of forgot."

"How could you forget something like this?" Julie shouts.

"Don't get me wrong, it was life-changing, but we were on the outside." I take a bite and put the roll down on my lap and take a sip of my beer. ok, it was 1978 or 79, I'm not sure. We were back from our navy tour. Caruso was in the police academy and I was starting in the insurance business. But we needed some work. (Turning to Caruso) I think your uncle on the police force got us the job to work security. Saturday Night Live felt like they needed extra security for one of their shows. They were short-handed, some of their previous security guards were acting more as fans than security. The job was only for Friday and all-day Saturday and possibly into the night after the show since there was always an after-show party. We took the job. We met at the NBC studios on Friday morning. We got assigned to look after the host, Eric Idle of Monty Python."

"This is unbelievable, how does this tie with a Beatle?" Julie shakes her head asking.

"I'm getting there. So, we get introduced to Eric and right away he notices we are not the usual security guard type. We are young, clean-cut navy types and not the serious security large bouncers. In between rehearsals, we would sit backstage and drink tea and get to know him.

He found our stories about being in the navy amusing. The rehearsals were done, and we had to follow him back to his apartment. The fans outside were crazy. Lots of pushing and shoving. This was after 'The Life of Brian' movie. There was a religious nut outside the NBC studio door and this guy threw a bottle at Eric and I caught it."

I take a bite of my sandwich.

"He caught it out of midair. It was great. We got into the limo with him and drove off to the apartment that they gave Eric to stay in for the week."

"So, we make our way up the elevator and Eric is still talking about the catch. He opens the door to the apartment and sitting on the couch, playing a ukulele, was George Harrison."

"You felt you never thought to mention this? For years I heard about some missing husband cases for hours, this he does not bring up." Joe is pissed.

"Why didn't we ever talk about this?" Caruso tries to remember.

"I'm not sure why we never spoke about this; we met a bunch of Yankees and had drinks with them a few times. That was more personal, this was working, and we were kids. It's not like we hung out with these guys."

I look around at the stunned faces in the boat. I am realizing that this was an important backstory of my life.

"Did you ever see these guys again?" Joe asks.

"Wait, you mentioned you met a TV star as well, who was that Johnny Carson?" Phillip throws the sarcastic statement at me.

"Oh yeah, I forgot. As we are standing in the foyer of the apartment with our mouths wide open Lorne Michaels walks into the apartment right behind us. I guess he is not a TV star, just the creator of Saturday Night Live."

"Was that the end of the night?" Asks a stunned Julie.

I look at Caruso, "Well, Eric walks up to George and tells him of the guy throwing the bottle and me catching it out of midair."

"And????" Joe screams.

"George asks what we did with the bottle and was there anything good in it."

Caruso laughs, "Then the night was over. Lorne Michael asks us to wait in the lobby. We headed downstairs and waited for two hours until he came back down and told us our night was over. We were not needed again. He did hand us a bottle of champagne from Eric."

"What a story. That was your fifteen minutes of fame." Phillip states.

Caruso looks around, "I think it's time we head back."

I head up front to pull the anchor in. Caruso starts the boat and pulls away slowly. I make my way to the back of the boat and sit between Joe and Julie. She has a smiling smirk on her face as she stares at me. "Anything else you're keeping to yourself?"

"Wait until he tells you about his ex-wife." Phillip gives up.

Joe bends over past me and gives Phillip a death stare. Phillip notices Joe's look, "Sorry Joe."

I am glad the time went by quickly as we hit Caruso's dock. The sun is going down. I jump up to help tie off the boat. Phillip hands me the cooler. Caruso turns off the boat, kills the lights and batteries. "I will rinse it down later. Let's watch the sunset with a drink. I have a good bottle of scotch in the house. JB, it's in the kitchen cabinet next to the fridge."

"Sounds like a plan, I 'll grab some glasses as well." I head into the house followed by Julie. I put the cooler on the patio.

"I bet it'll be hard to top that story unless your ex-wife stories are a real thrill." Julie laughs aloud as she helps herself to a few glasses.

I look at her, 'Four glasses only, Joe thinks this stuff tastes like iodine." I grab the scotch and walk back outside.

I open the scotch and pour four glasses. I go back to the cooler and grab a beer for Joe. I'm not sure what is so special about the sunset, but it always seems to take the conversation out of the air. We all click our drinks and stare at the blazing red ball until it's gone for another day.

Chapter 26

Wake or Funeral, Fun Times

I am up early and enjoying coffee down by the dock. This does not suck. Julie is the first to join me at the dock with coffee in hand.

"I guess we're the first up?" Julie asks.

"I thought I heard someone else up but all the doors are closed." Just as I finish, I hear the slider on the house open. Caruso is dressed for the day; he has a bag in his hand and coffee in the other.

"Muffins."

"I guess you were up and out early. Excited about your day?"

"There is nothing like a good wake to start your day."

I put a hand on Julie's back and steer her towards the muffins. I open the bag and hand one to Julie and one for Caruso. I take one for myself.

Caruso sits down, "Any idea what I will be looking for or who I will be looking for?"

"I would say anything that seems suspicious, but that's pretty stupid. Everyone looks suspicious to you."

Julie pipes in, "I would listen for names since you haven't met all the cast of characters, Miss Lee, Pamela Watson, or her father, …"

"Maybe our dear friend Jilly will show up. We should leave early and park close by so we can view the guest entering and give you some people to follow."

"Sounds good, we should leave here by 11 or so. Since it's only one time for the wake, there should be a good turnout." Caruso offers.

"I am going to shower and stir the other two for breakfast after I am done."

My phone goes off.

"Morning. What's up? (listening) We heard about the wake today. I don't feel very comfortable in those things. I think we'll avoid it. Will you be going? (Listening) OK, we need to check with the FBI this morning as well. (I frown and shake my head no-no.) OK talk soon."

"Copeland?" Julie asks.

"Yup, he is going to be at the wake, in the background he says. He is just one more person to be looking out for. We better take your car instead of our rental."

I head inside.

After a quick shower and shave, I dress and head back outside. Phillip and Joe are enjoying the sun.

"My turn." Julie states and heads in.

"JB, I'll stay here. I have a few things to handle with my publisher. I seem to be behind on my latest book."

Joe looks at him, "Latest book, did we know that you were writing again?"

"I owe them a book I promised a few years back. I think I now have enough material to put it together."

Caruso looks at Phillip, "What's it about?"

"Jamaica's life."

"I think that's a great idea." I offer proudly.

Caruso gets up, "I'm going to get ready to go. Phillip, the house is yours. We don't have much food here, plenty of coffee though."

"I need to shower; I'll be a quick Dad."

"Take your time."

Joe heads for the house, but stops and turns to me, "You know, something seems off with Pamela Watson. If you were supposedly on the run and fearing for your life, would you turn up at the school and follow me?"

I look at Caruso and Phillip. "I didn't think of that. You might have something there."

Joe turns and walks into the house, passing Julie.

"I threw all the towels by the washer," Julie tells Caruso.

"Thanks, as soon as Joe is ready, we'll leave."

CHAPTER 27

THE LONG AND WINDING ...
FUNERAL MARCH

"Joe you get in front, I'd rather be in the back to avoid anyone seeing me." We pile into Caruso's car and head for the wake.

We ride in silence for two hours, really, in silence.

Caruso pulls off the highway by the college. There's a two-lane highway circling the campus. We finally come across the funeral parlor. We drive around looking for a parking spot where we can watch the guest coming and going before Caruso goes in. Caruso finally picks a spot with a good view. His police training always comes in handy, I would have parked behind a big tree and seen nothing.

Within minutes we see two black limos pull up. A woman in a black dress gets out to carry a large box.

"Johnson, I presume?" I could not resist.

Everyone looks at me. "Come on, you were all thinking it. LOOK!"

"That's Miss Lee. She seems to be avoiding the lady with the box." I state.

More cars pull into the lot by the funeral parlor. There is a rush of mourners.

"Dad isn't that Pamela Watson."

We watch as Pamela greets Miss Lee very warmly. No one seems to pay any attention to them. A man dressed in a dark suit approaches both Pamela and Miss Lee and greats them warmly. The man holds onto their arms and steers them towards the door. Our suited man turns towards someone calling after him. From the driveway, I notice him, a small gray-haired man with a gray beard –

"Is that our albino?" Julie asks excitedly.

Caruso does a double-take trying to watch the action but also trying to comprehend what Julie just said.

I figured I would clear this up, "Copeland was trying to be funny at one point and stated they were following an albino from Canada in connection with this case.

"Dad, look over towards the stoplight, in the dark car."

"Copeland."

"We better stay out of sight. You ready to head in there?" Julie asks Caruso.

"What do you think if I leave my phone in my pocket and connected to you? You might be able to hear something."

"It might work. Good luck."

"When you put the phone in your pocket, put it in with the bottom of the phone at the top of your pocket. We'll hear the people better that way." Joe states.

Caruso takes the phone from his pocket and dials mine. He gets out of the car and makes his way straight to the funeral parlor. He walks to the front door and into the building. I can hear his breathing and lots of background noise. I hope this works.

Julie, Joe, and I keep a watchful eye on the front door and Copeland's car. I keep the phone's volume on high as we strain to listen.

I lean closer to the phone.

Joe whispers, "Dad put the phone on mute otherwise, he will hear us."

We hear Caruso talking to someone, "I met him a few times, this is awful……"

"Isn't that Miss Lee talking? It's getting louder, he must be getting close to her."

Loud and clear we hear Miss Lee talking to someone, 'This is my niece, Pamela.'

"Oh, Fuck. Did she just say that?" I let it fly in disbelief. I turn to Julie then to Joe.

"If this is true, this is a game-changer."

We hear Caruso moving around and multiple voices bouncing around the car. We hear a voice right next to Caruso.

'Dad, Dad…'

Julie looks at me, "That must be Pamela, and she must be right by Caruso. Boy is he good."

'Dad, can we go?'

We hear a muffled sound.

'Call me in a few days. I am leaving with my daughter.'

"Who was he talking with?" Joe looks at me.

"We'll wait for Caruso to give us a recap. This is amazing."

We see Copeland get out of his car and head towards the funeral parlor as Caruso heads out. He is wearing sunglasses. We hold our breath as they pass each other without even noticing each other. Caruso casually walks across the street and slowly towards his car. He looks both ways and gets into the car. We let out our breaths collectively.

He settles into his seat and his pause was worthy of an Academy Award. Julie and I are leaning so far forward that my nose was touching the windshield.

"WELL??" We all shout.

"I'm not sure you heard everything but it seems Miss Lee, Johnson's secretary is related to Pamela Watson. I'm thinking Pamela's dad and Miss Lee are brother and sister."

"This plays into your thoughts Joe," Julie states.

"Who was her dad talking with right before you left?" I must ask.

"Your Albino character, her dad was the only one who knew him. I never saw him on the line to pay his respects. We left at the same time but used the rear door that leads to the parking lot. Was that Copeland I passed on the way out? I can notice a good drip-dry suit anywhere."

"Now what?" Caruso asks.

Julie's phone rings. She quickly answers it. I try leaning over to see who is calling. She is very proper on the hello. It has to be Henderson.

"Yes sir, we're not getting anywhere. What have you got? (Listening for what seems like 20 minutes.) Julie has a puzzled look on her face. "Safe??" (More listening) "Ok, we will keep you informed if we find if something new.

I can come by the office in the next day or so. Yes, yes, I'll call first."

Julie hangs up and looks at me. "The FBI did a test on the safe from Johnson's office and found – nothing. The safe was empty."

"That doesn't surprise me after today?" Caruso asks as he starts the car and drives away.

We were silent driving here, I can't wait for the drive back to Caruso's house. The ride back goes quickly as the thoughts run through my head trying to piece this together. I feel I am close. I am daydreaming and working through my theory. Julie has fallen asleep on my shoulder.

Caruso's phone rings, Caruso looks at the number, "It's from my house, 'hello?'

(Listening) Jilly? Great. We should be there within twenty minutes." Caruso slams the phone into the cup holder.

"What's happening?" I ask.

"It seems Jilly has found out where I live, he must be tailing Forester who is also at the house. I'm glad I'm only renting this house."

"Sorry, buddy."

Now we drive in awkward silence. Regular silence was bad enough, not this. Julie starts opening her eyes and looks at me. "We need to stop Jilly from getting involved here. Especially since we are close, and he might not want us to be close."

"That's what I was thinking too. I'm not sure how to get rid of him yet."

"I was thinking Dad, can we get the FBI to pick him up? Henderson might not go for it since he knows what we're up to. Julie, maybe you might know a good friend who will go along with it?"

"Not bad idea, but after we pick him up where do we take him? How about Copeland, do we think he would help." Julie offers.

"Can you call Henderson and get the scoop on Copeland. Can we trust him? He is a federal marshal involved in a murder case. I think he's barking up the wrong tree now. Was this by accident or has someone been using him."

Caruso pulls onto his block, "Let's play along for a bit and get him out of the house. If need be one of you could walk away and call Copeland and get this in motion."

"Sounds like a plan," I state as the car stops and I get out. I walk into the house and the others follow. Jilly, Forester, and Phillip are sitting around the kitchen table drinking coffee.

Jilly gets up with an extended hand.

"Sorry to be here Captain, I never like to come to someone's house. Farante is missing, he was recovering from his wounds at home when his wife called. She came home from shopping and he was gone. I have worked with him for five years and we have never been out of contact with each other no matter how bad things get. I will leave you be, if you hear about where he could be, I'd like to be told."

Jilly lets go of my hand and pats me on the back. He seems terrified. He taps Joe on the cheek, "Be careful." We all watch him walk out the door.

"Who the heck was that?" I ask as if I never met him before.

"I have seen people scared before after a traumatic event in their life, but this guy was the last guy I would feel would be affected by a guy gone missing." Julie offers up.

I did not notice but Caruso went to his front window to see Jilly off. Caruso comes from the front of the house to the kitchen. "I think we just have seen an award-winning performance. He walked out of here all bent over and dejected as if someone ran over his puppy. He pulled out his phone, straightened up, and was very animated on his call. He put his phone back in his pocket and got into his car with a renewed energy."

"What do we think was behind the false story?" Joe asks.

"He was here awhile before we got back, how was he?" I ask.

"He was quiet, not like at the hotel the other day, all in charge." Phillip states.

"What brings you here again Bill?" Caruso asks as he removes his coat.

"I got another call from my buddy at the CIA, he called me from an outside line. As we expected, Jilly is CIA, Farante was CIA until he joined up with a hedge fund that has some offshore dealings as we also suspected."

"Nothing new there." I sound rejected.

"Nope, not at all, except Jilly and Farante never crossed paths in the CIA, they were brought together by someone who worked in the company for a few years in finance and accounting in Langley but quit for a better life as a......"

"Like a College President?" We all stare at Joe.

"How the hell did you surmise that?" Caruso blurts out.

"Lucky guess, but I did notice a diploma on the wall in his office from Virginia Tech in accounting. It also just hit me that the golf shirt Farante had on the day he got shot was from VT."

"He's smarter than you and I don't have to get him a gun permit," Caruso states proudly.

"That he is, that's why I wanted him as a partner. Do we think that there might be another safe, maybe in Miss Lee's office?"

"I think since tomorrow is Saturday it might be a quiet time on campus for us to look around," Julie says as she looks at us.

"I think we go tonight."

Everyone looks at me. "We're just there, and we are going to drive back?" Caruso stares at me.

"Exactly, no one will be around. We can take our time, no one will expect us."

"I am not sure this is a good idea." Forester admits.

"It's a good idea, but how do we get past locked doors?" Phillip asks me.

Before I answer, Julie jumps in, "I can take care of that. They had just typical deadbolts, pretty easy to get in."

Now we all stare at Julie.

Julie looks back and forth at us again. "We get taught all types of different hobbies along the way. Mine was picking locks."

"What about cracking safes?" Joe says sarcastically.

"It depends on the type," Julie says walking away from us.

The gang looks at me, "I knew nothing of these fabulous talents. OK, so we go tonight. I think we hit a nice restaurant on the water on the way up to the school." All eyes divert from me except Joe. "Yes, I'm paying."

"I don't think you need me any longer." Forester gets up to go.

"Not so fast Bill. Let's bring you up to speed from our wake surveillance. We now know that Pamela Watson, her dad, and Miss Lee are all related. Her dad and Miss Lee are brother and sister. What we don't know is how they tie into the missing money or their relationship with Johnson."

"We also do not know who the dangerous one is in the group. Someone is a killer or has contacts to hire one." Caruso states as he looks around the kitchen for something to eat.

"OK, now that I have been brought up to speed, what can I do? I have two weeks before I am full-time in my new job, and my navy retirement kicks in." Forester laments.

Everyone looks at me, I look at Joe.

Joe takes a deep breath, "We need to keep Jilly away from us. He seems to know our next move and always shows up when we don't want him to."

Julie walks back into the kitchen, "Maybe Henderson can help?"

"I have an appointment, so call me if I need to make a call. Remember you have all these different people watching you, CIA, FBI, Copeland, and a nasty group of bad guys. The odds are pretty good one of them will be joining you back at the school. If the bad guys are starting to panic, do you think they would have left something at the school and in a safe?" Forester heads for the door.

"He makes a good point." Phillip looks at me.

"Yes, he does. Though it doesn't mean we shouldn't head to the school and look around Miss Lee's office."

"You know how I told you that the former chief of detectives of NYPD is the mayor of this little hamlet here; well, he owes me big time. I think I'll visit him, and he can help dig into Pamela Watson's dad." Caruso offers.

"Lee, his last name is Lee." Blurts out Joe, "I was thinking his name was Watson, but Miss Lee is a Miss or so her nameplate on her desk says. So, if Pamela Watson's dad is her brother...."

"You're right; I was thinking it was Watson, which must be her maiden name. Nice deduction Watson." My failed attempt at a Sherlock joke.

"Ok, I'll head over to the mayor's house after I call him and you go do whatever you will do. I hate to say this Julie but let him take his gun. I know you have yours, but these people are a bit noisy. Jamaica remember this is not some abandoned New York City train yard, this is a college campus. Gunfire never goes over well."

"Understood, look, do me a favor, let us take your car, you take the rental." Julie gives me a death stare.

Caruso gets up and walks outside, he pulls out his phone to make the call to the mayor. We all watch him. He walks back in a minute.

"All set, Jones will see me. I'll call him from the car and we will meet at a local coffee shop instead of his house."

"He must owe you a big one?" Phillip asks.

"It's a long story. A case got messy. It involved his brother and the Mayor of New York City's wife. He could have lost his pension and his brother could have gone to jail. I thought the case stunk and dug deep on my own time and found out someone was trying to set up Jones and the Mayor."

"What a guy!" I could not resist. "Ok, let's get ready to go gang, we will meet back here later tonight."

Lots of stares, a pause, and finally everyone gets up and starts heading for their rooms to grab what they need. I follow Julie. She looks over her shoulder. "What?"

"I want to see these special tools for picking locks."

Julie walks faster into her room. She grabs her purse and turns to me. "Let's go."

"That's it?"

"Everything I need is in here including your gun which I will hold."

We all head out the door. Caruso throws me his keys as I do the same. Let them follow him.

CHAPTER 28

SHOW-DOWN

Julie takes the keys from me, she'll drive. It will give me time to think, probably out loud.

"Look, Joe nailed the theory that Pamela Watson, her dad, and Miss Lee are involved, but the question is how? We have been fed a lot of bits and pieces, especially from Jilly and the story about the ticket scam. Everyone showed us their hands, to a point. Even crispy Johnson who led us here was trying to show us something."

Julie looks over, "I agree, no one ever warned us off the case, they are all using us to piece this together."

"But why?" Joe asks, "Don't we think that the FBI, the federal marshal, and the CIA could solve this case without us?"

"Don't forget we were brought into this by Johnson who hired us under the premise that his football money was missing from some bowl game. Do we still think he was involved in the slush fund for college football?"

Phillip jumps in, "We found out the football game money was still at the school so Johnson had to figure we would find that out and the case would be over."

"Unless he was too scared. He needed a reason to call us. Was he over his head and had no way out? He couldn't go to the cops or the FBI with his story. Obviously, the CIA was not going to help a former agent. Maybe he was involved in both a college football slush fund and working with Farante on this giant ticket scam and CIA money." I offer to the gang.

Julie pulls the car off the highway into a restaurant parking lot facing the water. I have been talking for an hour straight it seems. She parks and we all get out. We walk up the wood plank deck around the back. The place is empty since it's late for dinner around here. No joke intended. The waitress sees us coming and waves us to any table which of course we take facing the water without any obstructions in our view.

We stop our conversation long enough to collect the menus from the waitress and to admire the water. It slows us down as we listen to the crashing waves. We order drinks and resume our theory.

"Maybe our dead client was playing both ends against each other." Phillip hopes.

"Or did some of the money go missing and he needed to replace it from the other pile of cash?" Julie states.

"I need to make a call, please order me a Cuban sandwich, no fries, thanks," I state and get away from the table. I walk towards the stairs leading to the sand. I call Caruso.

"We are good, …..stop that. We are getting food before going on. What did your friend find out? (Listening) That quickly he got that. (Listening) I get it, everyone owes something to someone. Yes me too. What? I had a hunch, that's why I called. OK. We will call as soon we are back in the car, or jail, whichever comes first." I hang up before he says something else. I pause and look at my cohorts at the table. I walk back to them.

Julie looks at me, "Anything we should know?"

"After dinner and in the car we can chat in the car. I had a hunch, and I was right."

"This cannot be a good hunch since you are patting yourself on the back," Philip says wearily.

I roll my eyes at him. The food arrives, we eat and enjoy the weather. I pay the bill and head for the car. I will drive from here. I motion to Julie for the keys. She gladly hands them over.

"This has to be serious, he is driving and will be talking too," Joe says worriedly.

"You know I need to send my car down here. A convertible is just the right thing to have down here with this marvelous weather." I say to no one.

"I just hope we get a chance to use it," whispers Phillip.

"I heard that…." After the doors close I look at my fearful group. "I had a feeling that Pamela was lying when she said her dad was a cop. I called Caruso who confirmed my thinking. It seems that Mr. Frank Lee is a computer consultant that works for the highest bidder. He is a hacker of renowned fame." I start the car and pull out of the parking lot and onto the highway.

Julie lets out an audible sigh. "You scared us to death back there like you found out he was some wanted killer."

I stare straight ahead. "He was a sniper in the special forces."

"Well, that sucks," Joe says as a matter of fact.

"He doesn't have a record that anyone can find."

"So, he has not been caught yet?" Julie states.

I need to get back on track. We'll be outside the school's neighborhood soon and I need a plan, plus my gun.

"What's next? What are we looking for in Miss Lee's office?" Phillip asks.

"I think any type of bank papers, wire instructions, account numbers, a little black book would be great and neat."

"Only in the movies does that happen." Julie laughs.

"You should know that most criminals are not very smart, or should I say most people are not very smart. Everyone needs to write their stuff down some...." I stop mid-word. I slowly pull into the parking lot of the administration building. There is still the police tape around the entrance and a patrol car parked out front. Over by the parking garage, standing next to his car on the second level holding a pair of binoculars is Copeland. I'm sure the FBI is here too somewhere. All we are missing are Miss Lee, her dangerous brother, and his lying daughter. I stop before entering the lot and drive past it. There's another entrance to the parking lot where Copeland is standing, I figure I would head there.

"You saw them too," Julie states. "Now what?"

"Jamaica, stop the car as you enter the garage and let me out." Phillip states. "No one notices the flunky of the world-famous detective. I'll sneak inside by walking right in. See you on the other side."

"Do you want my...."

"No, you shoot like crap, imagine me with that thing."

Phillip gets out of the car and slowly makes his way to a side entrance of the building. Everyone is stationed out front, he walks right in the side entrance. See most people are not very bright.

I look at Julie. "Who do we take our chances with Copeland or your boss?"

"Neither. Joe looks around back there, there has to be a golf hat of some sort, everyone down here carries a hat in their car."

Joe fishes out a cap from the back of the car from a bag. Joe finds a beat-up fishing hat and he hands it to Julie. She pulls all her hair up into it, grabs my sunglasses from the top of my head, and heads out the door. She walks back to my side of the car. I lower the window as I fish through her bag and remove my gun. I hand her bag back to her. Joe and I watch Julie enter the building through the same door that Phillip did.

I slowly drive up a level in the parking lot to where Copeland is hiding in plain sight. I notice he has an urgent manner to his stance. He is holding the binoculars with one hand and a radio in the other hand while talking rather loudly.

I turn to Joe. "Something seems wrong. Look." I point across the parking lot where Henderson has emerged from his car and is staring at the building.

"Joe, I think I prefer taking our case to Henderson right now. You drive to him and tell him that we are inside. I'm going to see if Phillip and Julie need my help."

Joe gets in the driver's side and backs out of the parking garage while I head to the side door of course.

I open the door and step inside the vestibule. I hear a loud voice behind me, "Hold it there."

I look up the steps and see a cop escorting Phillip down the steps with his hands up. Boy, I hope that the guy behind me is a good guy and not our sniper.

The cop nudges Phillip down the steps to where I am standing. "Let's go, both of you, outside." I look at Phillip with a quizzical frown. He shrugs and shakes his head no.

We are met at the side door by Copeland. "Did you think I would not see this character walking in the building? Why are you here?"

I can't process the fact why they saw Phillip but missed Julie. I look over at the parking lot and see Henderson talking with Joe. Since they are not making their way here I figure I am safe for now. I need to think fast.

"Why are you here, I believe I asked?"

"Something is bugging us about the football money. I wanted to look inside the safe. I know it got blown up but I figured there would be some remnants in the safe of something. (Knowing that the FBI already took the safe.) Johnson told me that he had money in the safe."

"Let's go back and look. I was hoping someone was going to come back here. I overheard someone at the wake say they wondered if there was more money hidden in the office. I felt it was worth a shot to watch out for it. Then you showed up."

Oh shit, we cannot go back there with Julie still snooping around. I hold my breath. We walk down the hall, past the police tape, and into the outer office, (oh yeah, the doors were unlocked. Some police investigation.) No sign of Julie. The two cops are standing by the door as Copeland, Phillip, and I have full rein in Miss Lee's office and Johnson's burnt office. Dumb luck.

All three of us head to where the safe should have been. I look at Copeland who looks at me. We both look at Phillip.

"I don't have it."

"Shit."

I need to look around the room, so I break away from the safe location. Phillip does the same and walks into Miss Lee's office.

I walk to the desk. "That is where we found Johnson, or at least what was left of him. But you know that. That explosion melted everything. The swords and that damn trophy got destroyed in the fire and the explosion."

I walk into the outer office. Phillip is standing by the sidewall. He taps his foot against the paneling, and I see it snap open slightly. He pushes closed.

Copeland walks out of Johnson's office. "Satisfied Biltmore? Let's get out of here."

Copeland does not wait for me; the other two officers follow him down the hall. Phillip hits the wall again. A hidden safe is revealed. He closes the paneling.

Phillip and I walk down the hall and outside. The two cops are long gone. Copeland is headed to his, he looks over his shoulder, "I will find out about the missing safe and call you." He does not wait for an answer as he gets into his car and pulls out of the garage. I wave to Joe who shakes Henderson's hand and gets in our car and heads for us. Now I need to find Julie.

Joe makes his way to us. I keep looking around for Julie. I hear the door to the building opening.

Julie stands there with a smirk on her face. "I will walk the other way, so Henderson doesn't see me. Pick me up in the parking garage."

"Where were you?"

Julie stops and looks back at me, "In the lady's room. Guys feel extremely uncomfortable looking in there."

I walk with Phillip to Joe and get into the car.

"Pull back into the garage. We need to pick up Julie." I see Julie at the far end of the parking garage between two cars. Joe pulls the car to the other end of the garage and Julie jumps into the back seat.

Joe looks at me, "Where shall I go?"

"We passed a coffee shop on the way here right outside the campus, we can park in the rear lot and gather our thoughts. We have a lot of things to talk over."

Joe pulls out of the parking garage and makes his way onto the road that circles the campus.

I point to the coffee shop with the large parking lot, "Pull around back."

Joe pulls in and parks in the rear, he backs into a spot, "Just so we can see if anyone approachs."

"Smart."

"I will run in, obviously wearing this hat and sunglasses work. What does everyone want?"

"Iced tea."

"Same"

"Coffee with milk please."

Julie gets out. She goes into the shop and within 5 minutes she is out with our drinks. She gets back in the car.

"Ok, who wants to start?" I look around.

Joe jumps in, "The only reason Henderson was there was because he had an agent follow Copeland at the wake. He saw you and Phillip going into the building and figured he was right to be following Copeland. I told him we were there because we wanted to see the office again looking for missing clues. I told him we were at a dead end."

I haven't heard a thing he said. Something hit me that is so impossible, but I cannot get it out of my head.

"I met Phillip at the office door and opened the lock. We were able to look around for a minute or so before Copeland showed up. Phillip found the second safe quickly though it was locked. Once we heard Copeland coming, I ran out a side door towards the ladies' room. Once you and Phillip left the office again, I went back inside." Julie recounts.

"Anything strike you funny?"

Phillip stares at me, "Oh no, you picked up something didn't you?"

I take a sip of my coffee.

"Dad?"

"Jamaica?"

"OK, everything in Johnson's office got burned pretty well. His desk, his chair, the bookcase, his globe, they all looked awful."

Julie leans forward from the back seat towards me, "We all saw it, and smelled it. Everything was burnt, we get it."

"That damn football trophy and his swords were no-where in sight."

"Maybe the heat melted them to a point where they lost their shape." Phillip offers.

"No way. I was still able to recognize the globe, it was flat and black, but you can see the map."

"Do you think someone stole them, Dad?"

"I do not."

"OK Jamaica spill the beans, what are you thinking?" An annoyed Phillip asks.

"I think someone took the swords and trophy out of the room before the fire."

"So, you think the fire and the explosion were set on purpose and someone removed the sword and trophy so they wouldn't get ruined in the fire?" Julie states.

"Miss Lee?" asks Joe.

"Johnson." I throw out for the gang to swallow.

"Wait a minute, you think Johnson is still alive?" Julie asks in amazement.

"I do."

I look around the car at the stunned faces. Philip has a smirk on his face.

"Do you have this all worked out in your head?" Phillip asks.

"I don't. This hit while we were in the office and I saw those items missing. Why would they be missing unless someone purposely took them out? His timing had to be perfect. We were in his office, then left for a tour of the campus then came back. This was staged. I'm guessing that Miss Lee is involved too. I'm not sure if this is one big group of thieves or different groups working different ends."

"Where do we go now, Dad?"

"Jamaica, why were we brought in? Do you think Johnson saw an opportunity to escape with the money but needed us to help with the scheme?"

I look at Phillip, "Maybe. We have a large cast of characters and we need to think about who is working with whom, what money is missing, and who has it."

157

Julie shakes her head, "The way I see it, this money has been untraceable for years. Why do we think we will be able to figure out where it is now?"

"I think we have two very separate groups here."

"Dad!"

"Let's think about everyone we have met…"

"Dad!"

Joe does not wait for an answer. He hits the gas and rams the side of a late model sedan. A gunshot goes off. We were parked and drinking our coffee and iced teas so we all bounce around the inside of the car. Julie is out of the car behind her door, gun out. She reaches over the car seat where I am between the seat and the dashboard. She hands me my gun. Joe smartly ducks down.

There is no movement in the car, I look over my door and slowly make my way over to the car. There is a large bloodstain on the windshield.

People are running for cover from the parking lot and the coffee shop. I am sure we will be hearing sirens soon.

I get up from my crouched position; I put my gun in the waistband of my pants. As luck would have it when Joe rammed the car the guy in the driver's side of the car was about to shoot but the jolt somehow sent him against the door violently and he shot himself in the head. I wouldn't believe it if I did not see it either. Julie makes her way to the guy to get the gun away from him just in case. Good training.

As expected, the parking lot fills up quickly with police cars. They are out of their cars quickly with guns drawn, crouching behind the doors of their cruisers. Since this is not New York, I put my hands up. Out on the road in front of the coffee shop, I see the familiar, unmarked car of Copeland come screeing into the lot. He jumps out of the car, badge in hand.

"Federal Marshal. Stand down."

One of the cops who is the ranking officer looks at Copeland. "Let's see the ID." He turns to another officer, "Go check on the guy in the car."

Julie and I walk over to him. Julie shows him her ID.

"Hey Sarge, she is FBI. Oh, and the guy in the car is dead."

"He shot himself." I offer. The officer looks at me and then at Julie. Julie has the guy's gun in her hand hanging off her little finger to save fingerprints. She is good.

"He did shoot himself. I never fired and you can smell his gun." She holds it out to the officer.

The sergeant and Copeland are chatting and walk their way over. "Mr. Biltmore."

"Copeland."

"What happened?"

"We took a break and decided to have a coffee while enjoying the sunshine. This guy came into the lot driving like a nut. I was on the driver's side of the car and I must have never put the car in park, so when this guy came into the lot it surprised me and I guess I hit the gas and hit his car causing the poor fellow to shoot himself in the head."

Copeland stares at me, looks at the car with Philip still in the back seat and Joe standing next to the car. He looks at Julie.

"Agent Waters, is this how you see it?"

159

"Pretty much."

"OK, I will let you report this to your boss as you see fit. Mr. Biltmore let's take a walk. You will need a tow truck I presume," Caruso states.

"Dad, Caruso's car is a mess."

Phillip sticks his head from the car, "I will call him."

Julie walks away and makes a call.

"This is all well and good, but I need to fill out a lot of paperwork." The Police Officer states with much annoyance.

"We can make this a federal case and you assisted so the paperwork becomes my issue. I will call this in," Caruso says.

"Suits me. I will leave a car here to wait for the morgue and the tow trucks."

Copeland makes a call to his office.

The sergeant motions for the other police cars to leave the area. He goes to his car, gets a roll of yellow crime scene tape, throws it to the officer he is leaving behind, "Until the feds show up, this is still a crime scene. If they are not here in one hour call me back and we take over."

A young man from the coffee shop comes over to the sergeant. "What are we supposed to do?"

"I will have a regular coffee, get everyone else whatever they want. That guy, (pointing to me) is buying." The Sergeant says.

Phillip walks over with his phone. "He wants you."

I take the phone and walk away from the crowd, "We were parked. Joe saw the guy coming into the lot with his gun sticking out the window, he thought fast and rammed the guy causing the guy to shoot himself – I swear he did. I never even pulled my gun. (Listening)

160

Your car is in bad shape. This was an ugly car anyway. No, you cannot use my Vette, plus it's not here yet. (Listening) Yeah, it is funny now. Hey, by the way, I think Johnson is still alive. Talk later." I hang up. The phone rings. "Yup, still alive. (Listening) Only us, Copeland showed up here. It was rather fast right?? OK, talk later. Oh, I think we need a ride. Do you want to come to hang out with us? Come on it will be fun. We are getting close; people are taking better shots at us! I figured since you have my rental car, it will bring Jilly here since there has to be a GPS tracker in the car. See you soon, we will call you. I need to talk with Copeland."

I hand the phone back to Phillip; I need to chat with Copeland."

Copeland and Julie are chatting by the cars. Fractured Fairy Tales time.

Copeland sees me coming over, Julie walks away.

A young girl comes out of the coffee shop with an order pad, "I will take a coffee, again, Copeland?"

Copeland looks at the girl, "I'll have the same."

I look at her, "Please get them something as well." The girl goes to the police officer then Julie, Joe, and Phillip. Copeland and I move further away from the group.

"Ok Mr. Biltmore. I'm figuring you are getting close since this was not someone sending a message. Care to share what you have?"

"We were looking for anything in the office that looked out of place, that's all we got."

"I am sure you noticed that the football trophy was missing from the office?"

I gulp.

"I think someone walked away with it. I know the FBI has taken the safe to review the contents, you would not have heard any results from their test?"

"Matter of fact, we have. They said it was empty. You and I found the football bowl money the other day, we think Johnson lied to us, we are trying to figure out why."

"Who is your client?"

"You do not want to know." I refuse to say.

"Run it past me."

"Confidentially, the FBI is paying our expenses."

"Expensive case, 2 cars, a few dead bodies and I cannot wait for the rest. Oh, since Miss Waters is with you, I figured she was hiding in the building when I picked up you and your buddy there. I did see your son talking with Henderson too."

"You are good."

"Why are you dragging him into this, a nice college kid? Let him have his fun. There will be plenty of time for this crap."

"Good point. Hey, you have leveled with me, try this on for size, I think Johnson is still alive." What did I just do? I think I trust this guy. I am sure it will backfire.

"Excuse me?"

Shit, I need to go all-in now, "The trophy and the swords from his wall are all missing. Johnson loved these things, I am figuring he set this all up, so he took this stuff before blowing up some other guy."

"Now what?"

"We don't know, I usually do not plan these cases out, they kind of just fall into place."

"Where do we go from here? You have no car."

"We are waiting for a ride."

"Your buddy from the NYC police department won't be here for two hours. You probably need to lay low for a bit."

"How did you know about him?"

"Remember my badge says, Federal Marshal."

"Oh, why are you involved, besides the albino story?"

"We only got involved because we had a warrant for a certain money launder that used to work for the CIA."

"Farante."

"Farante. Where can I drop you and your little team?"

"Not sure."

A tow truck comes to grab Caruso's car. They hook it up, Phillip walks over and takes care of the paperwork including the credit card required. The driver of the tow truck hands Phillip his card. He cannot help staring at the blood-splattered body in the other car. "I have seen a lot of accidents and no way did you hit him that hard to cause that."

The tow truck driver gets back in his rig and gently pulls away with Caruso's car. Julie, Joe, and Phillip are now sitting under a large palm tree sipping their drinks waiting for me.

I have an idea of a location that should keep us safe as I head over to them. "Julie, can you make a call?"

CHAPTER 29

SETTING A TRAP

Copeland pulls up to the airplane hangar.

I open my door, "We'll hang out here. Once Caruso gets closer, I'll call you. I'm sure he is being followed. I'm not sure how we are going to get all the bad guys in one place."

Copeland calls from the car, "You have a way of attracting only the best of the worst. Oh, please do everything possible not to use that gun of yours."

Copeland pulls away from the hangar. We quickly head to a side door that is open as to not stay outside too long.

The hangar's lights are off. We hear a car come screeching to a stop outside. Julie and I pull out our guns, "I'll get the lights Dad."

"Leave them off."

The overhead door starts opening up which scares the shit out of us. Standing in the doorway is Henderson with the sun beaming behind him making him look even larger.

"Put those things away." He pulls out a door clicker and the overhead doors close.

My new philosophy is to tell everyone we meet exactly what I am thinking about the case. Someone must be bad.

Henderson looks at us. "Give it to me straight, did this guy shoot himself?"

"He did. I don't think that was his intention, but that is how it ended for him."

"Let's go sit and tell me everything you have. We are wasting a lot of government money on this case. I have a feeling at the end we will be told to just drop it." Henderson walks into the same room that we have been in before. This time we all help ourselves to the water. Henderson turns on the AC.

Julie looks at me and nods her head towards Henderson.

"I think Johnson is still alive."

Henderson dribbles some water out of his mouth and wipes it with his shirt sleeve. "Come again?"

"As you know we were back in his office today, both the trophy and his matching swords are missing, nowhere in sight. I realize this is a hunch, but we found another safe as well. The safe was hidden behind some panels in Miss Lee's office. We never got inside but we also think that Miss Lee is involved as well."

"OK, let's say this is right. Why bring you down here?"

"We think it was a cover-up. We do think Johnson was involved in some type of college slush fund that distributed money to different schools to pay these kids and their families. We think this was an organized group."

"Remember we never found any trace of any burnt money in the safe."

"We do."

"Did someone steal the bowl money as he said?"

"Nope, the school has that money sitting in another account, which money has always been there."

"How did you find that out?"

"We asked."

"I wish we thought of that."

My cell phone goes off. I take it out of my pocket. Forester. I hit the end and put it back in my pocket.

"Look, sir, we don't have much more. We have a cast of characters but no way to tie them together. We cannot prove anything, especially the slush fund at this point." Julie offers.

My phone goes off again, I remove it from my pocket, Forester.

"Mr. Biltmore, take your call."

I hit the green button and walk away from the group. "What's up?" (Listening) I need to use all my powers to not look at Henderson and Julie talking. "(I Whisper) Are you out of your fucking mind? I don't know, some FBI airplane hangar. OK."

"All good Dad?"

"Yeah, the tow truck company said the insurance company does not want to cover the repairs until they hear from Caruso. He is going to be pissed. I should call him and tell him where to pick us up. Where exactly are we?"

"Tell him to pick you up at the school. I think we should head there and see if this safe has anything that will help us." Henderson says.

"Sure. Sounds like a plan. Whatever you think will work."

Phillip and Julie are not buying my cooperation. Henderson gets up and is the first one out the door, he opens the overhead door, and we follow him out to his car. Three in the back will be tight.

"Phillip, you sit in the front." I want to have my gun handy. Something smells.

"Dad, text Caruso and tell him where we are headed, he should almost be here." I make a motion for him to give me his phone. I take it.

I text Julie and Joe – FORESTER HAS SEEN AN INTERNAL MEMO FROM THE NCAA TO THE NFL ABOUT MILLIONS OF MISSING FUNDS EAR MARKED FOR EXPENSES. HENDERSON'S EXPLANATION IS NOT HOLDING UP.

"I better call him instead." I dial Caruso on Joe's phone. "Hey, we are headed back to Johnson's office. Meet us there. Oh, by the way, your car is like the Met's last season – dead on arrival."

Henderson laughs.

Henderson pulls his car into the same lot we were in a few hours ago. He parks, we get out. I adjust my gun. Julie notices and removes her gun and puts it into her pocket. Joe notices and walks behind us at a safe distance.

We walk into the building and down the hall to Miss Lee's outer office. We hear voices.

Henderson holds out his hands for us to stop. Down a side hallway, I see Caruso hiding in a doorway alcove.

I hear a noise coming from the stairwell next to us. I see a large pair of shoes, Jilly.

I tilt my head towards Caruso and Jilly. Phillip and Julie see both of them. Joe starts walking back toward the door. Probably a smart move.

Henderson motions to us to move back towards the door. I see Caruso has that look on his face – no what?

We quietly walk back outside and smack into Forester. Henderson grabs us and hustles us off away from the doorway.

"Get going behind these cars."

We split up and crouch behind two cars watching the front door. Henderson looks at Forester, "And you are?"

"Bill Forester."

"Nice to meet you, Admiral."

Joe looks at me, "You left your phone on didn't you so Uncle Bill can trace you?"

FBI Henderson's head swings toward the door as Miss Lee, her brother, and our short gray-haired guy walk out.

"Henderson, he is tied in with these guys." FBI Henderson says in wonderment.

My head does a Linda Blair. I stare at Forester.

"The memo just said Henderson. What are the odds." Forester says sheepishly.

"A relative?" I ask.

Henderson laughs.

"What's our plan?" Julie asks.

I think whatever our plan was it just changed. Jilly walks out the doors and surprises Lee and Lee and Henderson standing at the steps. Jilly shakes the hand Henderson. Jilly will either cause a firefight or steer this group away from the area. Shit, he is leading them back into the school.

Now what?

"I don't think we have time for backup, plus as of now no one has done anything wrong that we know of." Henderson offers.

"I am not sure any of these people are killers so if I go in we can see where this goes," I suggest.

"Dad, they did try and kill us at the coffee shop."

"Someone has Farante, for what reason?" Julie asks.

"I'm not sure the killer is in this group," I say with no conviction.

"I'd feel better if Agent Waters went in with you."

Julie looks at me and shrugs. "Why not? Do you have a plan once we scare the hell out of them?"

"I do not, do you?"

Julie laughs. "Let's go."

Julie and I get up from behind the car and start walking towards the building. I grab Julie's hand. I look at her, "We need to find another line of work."

"Tomorrow."

We walk into the school. "Where the hell is Caruso?" I look around.

We walk into Miss Lee's office through the partially open door. I notice that the safe is open. The conversation in progress comes to a halt.

"Mr. Biltmore, we were not expecting you." Miss Lee states.

Mr. Lee has a menacing look on his face, ex-snipers usually do. He reaches inside his sport coat. Jilly puts a strong arm on Lee's.

Jilly smiles, "Hello Special Agent Waters."

"Jilly."

"Can we help you Jamaica?" Jilly ask.

"Well to be honest we were hoping to have a chat with whoever keeps shooting at us. I hate when that happens. Oh, by the way, the guy at the coffee shop today shot himself in the head with a .45. Do you know what does at close range, and in a car? The resale value will drop instantly. (I turn towards Henderson and figure I would shock him.) Mr. Henderson, I presume?"

Henderson looks at the Lees and Jilly.

"So, I noticed earlier today that Johnson's swords and dear football trophy are missing." I throw out there to see where it will stick.

Miss Lee looks around trying to relax, "We noticed the same thing."

I see a pair of feet by the side door.

"Where is he?" I ask looking around the office.

"Who?" Miss Lee innocently asks.

"Johnson."

"Look, Mr. Biltmore, his ashes will be spread around the football stadium on Saturday. I am not sure what you are saying." Miss Lee states almost convincingly.

I chuckle.

"Do we know if the dead guy even likes football?"

Jilly laughs. Jilly lets hold of his grip on Mr. Lee who pulls out a gun from his coat.

Julie gets her gun out, Mr. Lee now points his at her giving me time to take mine out. Caruso walks in the side door with a gun drawn. I tilt my head towards Caruso. Everyone looks at him. Mr. Lee drops his gun.

"This is why we never carry guns. It always gets messy." Jilly says laughing.

"Look Jamaica, I have told you everything I know about the case including Farante being taken from his house. I know it sounds silly, but I am on your side."

I look cockeyed at Jilly.

"Well maybe not on your side per se but I am not against you."

"That's fair."

"Where do we go from here? We both know that the Lees' have not done anything they can be charged with besides holding a gun on a federal agent." Jilly offers.

"Well, that is enough to hold them for quite some time while we sort this out, at least no one will be shooting at us."

"Sure we will have a few scapegoats, but this will never see the light of day." Jilly states matter of fact.

"I am not so sure about that. Do you mind letting us in on what was in the safe?"

"Not really. This is my safe in my office. The contents belong to me." Miss Lee says firmly.

"That's not true. The contents belong to the school." Caruso interjects.

"Never mind. Jilly is one regard you are a client. Are we done here?"

Julie and Caruso look at me.

"We are," Jilly says unsure of my motive.

"Ok let's go." I look at Julie and Caruso.

I back out of the door and pull Julie with me. She is not happy. She turns on me as soon as we are out the door.

"What the hell."

Caruso is looking at me. "What are you up to?"

Julie looks at Caruso, "How did you know we were in trouble?"

"When he references the Mets, it means trouble."

"We'll talk outside," I state.

Henderson, Joe, and Phillip see us and walk out from behind the car. They too have a puzzled look on their face.

"What happened in there?" Henderson asks angry.

"Something is wrong. I can't put my finger on it." I walk away from the group. Everyone is staring at me. My mind is racing, I think Johnson was the holder of the slush fund money for college football. I think he told Miss Lee everything about the fund and about a different kind of fund set up fifteen years ago while he worked as an accountant for the CIA. That's where he worked with Farante, a known money launderer but useful to the CIA. So, Miss Lee tells her brother about both funds. They decide to go after the big money. Being a computer hacker, Mr. Lee helps himself to millions of dollars in CIA money. Farante who is still running this massive fund for both the CIA and whoever needs it gets wind of the money disappearing from the accounts in Cuba. But how does this get tied into the college slush fund?"

Julie has walked over to me and surprises me when she grabs my arm. "What's wrong?"

"I am not sure. It's simple and that worries me. I know we can bring the Lees in for a shit load of charges but it's being tied up too easily. It's all there for us. Someone has gift-wrapped this for us."

"Jilly, Dad?"

"I was thinking that myself. I'm not sure though. Someone is making sure we bring down everyone at once, the Lees, short Henderson, Farante, Johnson, and maybe Jilly."

"Mr. Biltmore, I need to get going. Are we done here?" Henderson says impatiently.

"I think so."

"Where are you headed?" Henderson asks but not caring.

"I am not sure." I look at my gang. "Our hotel is only about twenty minutes from here. Do you want to join us for dinner?"

Henderson looks at all of us. "Sure, what the heck."

I look at Julie, "We'll go with Caruso. Phillip, can you take Joe and go with Bill? We'll meet at our hotel."

CHAPTER 30

AS PLAIN AS THE NOSE....

Caruso cannot help staring at me.

"What?"

"Do you realize that the insurance company is giving me a hard time about the car? When Sarah gets back, she will blow a fit." Caruso states.

"I will talk with her. She loves me."

"I do not know why." Caruso shakes his head.

"We are like family."

"You are family, you idiot."

Julie hits me from the back seat. "What does that mean?"

"She's my sister."

"I learn so much about you every day." Julie sits back exhausted.

"Wait." Caruso chuckles to himself. He looks at me. "Are we expecting Jilly to follow us?"

"I would hope so. I do not think he will be bringing the Lee siblings. They do not seem like a fun family."

"I wonder where the daughter is, I kept on thinking about her during our little meeting. Do you think she and Johnson were involved?" Julie asks with eyes closed resting her head on the headrest in the back seat.

"I didn't until now. Are we missing someone in this mess, or is this easily wrapped up?" I ponder.

"You know all of this will go away and be swept under the table unless we prove the football slush money is real. No one will care about the CIA slush fund, it to convolute anyway. Caruso states emphatically.

My phone rings in my pocket, I reach for it. I do not recognize the number, but I answer it anyway.

"Hello? (Listening) OK, why should I care that you have Farante?" (Listening)

I cover the phone and turn to Julie, "call Joe quickly."

Julie pulls out her phone and dials quickly, she puts her hand over the phone to mute her voice, "Joe?" Julie looks at me stunned.

"What do you want? (Listening) a trade? What could we possibly have that you want? You have Farante and my son. (Listening) Why do you think I have the power to have the Lees' taken into custody?"

Julie is listening to the entire conversation on her phone which is still connected to Joe's phone. She keeps Joe's phone connected while she dials Henderson, tall Henderson. We are facing each other trying to listen to each other plus Johnson on the other end.

I motion Caruso to pull over onto the side of the road which he does quickly. Julie steps out to take her call.

"I'm listening, so if we get those two out of the way you will release Joe? That's all you need. You do know everyone knows you are alive right?" Caruso slaps my arm.

"What type of proof do you need? OK. Give me twenty minutes. I will call this number." I hang up. "Fuck."

Julie gets back in the car, "It seems Johnson was waiting for them at the hotel as they got out of the car, he grabbed Joe and threw him in his car, and sped off."

Caruso pulls back into traffic heading for the hotel which is only a minute or two away. I have no idea how we will now find the Lees, especially if Jilly left them. We pull into the hotel parking lot. Henderson is on the phone.

Caruso parks and we get out. Forester rushes over, "We could not stop him."

Henderson walks over while still on the phone. "Sorry, I got here a minute too late. I called in the make and model of the car I got from Phillip here."

Phillip looks at me, "There was a woman in…"

"Pamela," I state.

"How did you know?" Phillip asks.

"Julie figured it out. We need to figure out how to get the Lees off Johnson's tail. I am guessing that is what has him so worried."

"I got an idea." I get my phone and dial Jilly. I do not wait for his hello. "I figured you were going to meet us at the hotel. I need to find out where the Lees are. Johnson was at the hotel waiting for us and took Joe as he got out of his car. Johnson wants us to get the Lees in custody before releasing Joe. I am not so sure this guy is on the up and up. After all, he killed some guy in his office and I figure he is behind us getting shot at. (Listening) OK. Call me when you have them."

"Jilly will grab the Lees and call us when he has them."

"That is all well and good Mr. Biltmore, but I would like my team to chase this down as well. I think you might be better off with us getting your son back. Jilly is a wild card." Henderson offers.

"Agreed."

Henderson gets in his car and takes off. He doubles back and opens his window. "Use the hangar if you need a safe place." Henderson throws me the overhead door clicker.

I turn to the group, "Where would Johnson feel safe enough to take Joe?"

Everyone stares at the ground.

"Oh my god." Julie stares at the phone in her hand. Her hands are shaking, she dropped the call to Henderson but not to Joe who is still connected. Julie hits the speaker button, and we hear a faint narration of the car ride.

Julie makes sure the call is still on mute. We hear a conversation between who we think is Pamela and Johnson. 'Just keep driving, we will stop at your office and get those account papers. I don't care about my dad and his crazy-ass sister. This got out of hand. I just want my share of the money. I have a flight lined up to get me out of here. I will leave you and this college kid after I know I am in the clear."

"Call Henderson, tell him to get to the school. Let's go."

We pile into Caruso's car, or should I say my rental car. Caruso will drive.

"Stop, everyone out. We will take Forester's car."

Everyone gets out and hurries over to Forester's car. We take off out of the hotel parking lot.

"No GPS tracking device," I say to no one in particular.

Forester drives as fast as he can without being noticed.

"Do I call Copeland?" I ask turning to Julie.

"I guess, it can't hurt."

I dial Copeland, "Hey, Johnson took Joe, and we think he is headed to the school to get some papers from Miss Lee's office. Pamela Watson is pulling the strings. Thanks, see you there."

One more call.

"Jilly, it's Biltmore. They are headed to the school. There must be something in the office that Pamela wants."

Caruso looks back at me from the front seat, "You know this has the chance to be a blood bath right?"

"I am hoping between Henderson and Copeland this gets worked out." Everyone looks at me.

"I know, stupid thought. So, Bill, how's retirement doing?"

"The navy was easier, if we got in trouble we called in the North Atlantic fleet and things got settled. This is crazy shit."

Forester pulls into our parking lot; it seems like ours. Maybe we can get our name on the football stadium when this is done. Forester cuts his lights.

"Maybe there is another door we can use to get into the building. Do you have your little tools to get into the building?"

"I do." States Julie.

Caruso looks at me, "I say we split up. Bill, you come with me. If the shooting starts you have a better chance with me than with him."

Caruso and Bill head around the building to find another way in. In the distance I see Henderson. Right now he seems to be alone. He is headed for the door we have used before. No imagination.

I hear an approaching car, Copeland. Driving with his lights off, he passes the entrance to the parking lot and goes into the parking garage. He loves that place.

Julie and I head to another side door where she can work her magic on the lock. I turn and notice Phillip staring into space.

Whispering, "What is it?"

"I was thinking of the stateroom scene in Night at the Opera. If one person panics, we will all be inside. I will stay out here; I hope Forester left his key in the car. Phillip walks over to the driver's side and leans in. He pops his head out and gives me the thumbs up. I turn and Julie is already at the opened door waiting for me. I hustle over.

Julie and I enter the building. The night lights are on, I remove my gun and Julie does the same. I look around and I am lost.

"Nothing looks familiar."

Julie shakes her head. "We need to go upstairs. This door and the door we have used before are on different elevations from outside."

Julie does not wait for me, she jogs up a flight of stairs with me close behind. We reach the top of the stairs. The voices from the end of the hall echo in the empty building. There is a lot of shouting going on.

Looking down the dark hall we see Henderson enter the office with his gun drawn. Approaching from another corridor is Copeland, his gun is drawn also.

I look at Julie, I take off in a full sprint. Caruso, crouched in a recessed doorway, sees me and joins me in my sprint. Julie is right behind me.

It seems like an hour before we get to the office. I stop right before entering. I motion Caruso to head to the side door he had used before. I take a deep breath and Julie and I burst into the room. God, I don't want to get shot, it really hurts.

Chapter 31

WHO THE F ARE YOU??

I am the first through the door. Caruso follows through from the side door. Forester is behind him. I pull Julie behind me, instinct I guess, she is not going to be happy I did that. I survey the room.

Johnson is wandering around his blackened office.

Miss Lee is seated at her desk and her brother is sitting on the desk.

Pamela is leaning against the opened door that leads to Johnson's office.

Henderson, the tall one, still has his gun trained on someone while standing in the middle of the room.

Copeland, sweating like a mad dog which he is right now, is standing next to the doorway that Caruso is standing in.

I'm still in a panic looking for Joe. My head must be bouncing back and forth since I missed him. Julie grabs me and points to Joe sitting on the window ledge drinking water with a shitty grin on his face.

Johnson comes from his office with an extended hand, "Mr. Biltmore, nice to see you again. Sorry about taking your son. It was a matter of national security."

I look around the room. I hand my gun to Julie.

"Let me guess, everyone here works for the government in some capacity?"

Johnson looks around the room, "It seems so."

"This is so messed up," Copeland says in disgust.

"Talk about a waste of money." Big Henderson says about to leave.

I need to ask, "I don't get why someone was trying to kill us. This last guy in the parking lot came close. If Joe didn't act so quickly, I think one of us would be dead. There is a silence around the room. Everyone is staring at each other.

"Dad, do you realize we are still missing Farante, Jilly, and small Henderson?"

I didn't notice. "Are these missing guys part of someone's agency, or do we have a couple of rogue agents on our hands?"

Silence.

"That's what I thought. Oh, by the way, which bundle of money were you chasing?" I look first at Johnson.

"The CIA slush fund," Johnson states.

"Were you part of the CIA at one point and did you work with Farante?"

"Very good Mr. Biltmore, I'm impressed," Johnson says smugly.

"Joe figured that out. Lees, are you related and what money were you following?" I ask.

"The CIA money, we are NSA, we are brother and sister." Miss Lee confesses.

I turn to Pamela, I put my hand up, "Joe, Call Phillip, he needs to hear this. Miss Watson, what are you chasing?"

"I am not at liberty to say." Pamela proudly states.

Everyone laughs at her. Pamela looks around. "Ok, I am with Navy Intelligence."

"Bill, she is one of yours. Pamela, meet Admiral Forester."

Henderson looks at me, "Someone shot this guy Farante, and someone shot at you in your hotel. Something still stinks here."

"So, no one is looking for some missing NCAA slush fund?" I almost forgot.

Silence.

Johnson looks at me. "Guilty, I was involved in both I guess you can say."

"Who was the dead guy in your office?" Julie asks.

"I have a friend at the funeral parlor across the street. He was going to be cremated anyway."

"Continue." I sound pissed.

"I called you in because there was some money that went missing. I heard about this supposed slush fund used to pay off athletes and their families. I was approached by a few boosters after we won our game. They asked if I would help keep track of the money. They knew my background as an accountant. I helped them set up these various accounts. Then the money went missing. I still don't know where it is but I suspect Farante took it." Johnson admits.

"Yeah, our bad, I was in some of those meetings with Johnson and the boosters. I saw all the accounts and how they were set up. We heard Farante might have a lead on the CIA money. He has been a suspect to us for years. Johnson here refused to help Farante move some of the CIA money, so we figured if we helped Farante steal the football money he would lead us to the CIA slush fund. Farante thought that stealing the football money would get Johnson motivated, instead it got this nut to blow up his office." Miss Lee says.

"We were following Henderson and we would have had him until Copeland screwed that up. Henderson was one of us for years and somehow met Farante and hooked up with him." Pamela offers up.

Copeland stares at her, "Biltmore and his group have been less trouble on this case than you bunch of amateurs."

Copeland walks out of the office and I follow him. The door closes, "Are you at all surprised that Jilly is not here?" I ask.

Copeland looks at me, "Shocked. Call me later."

I go back inside. I think it's time to wrap this up.

I look at Henderson, "Since you all work together not much more we can do here." I start to walk out but turn around.

"If we get shot at again or my son gets taken again, I will blame someone in this room. Remember I have an Admiral on my side and Joe here has an Uncle back in New York who will not look kindly if something happens to Joe." I wave to Joe, Phillip, Caruso, and Forester to follow me. I open the door and walk into the hallway followed by the group.

Caruso laughs aloud, "Quoting the Godfather now that is priceless."

My phone rings, I answer it and stop in my track. The others keep walking except Julie.

"I was expecting you to make an entrance. (Listening) (Interrupting Jilly) You know they will find you. Do not play dumb, you had someone take shots at me, even if they were meant to miss us, the last one was not going to miss, was he? (Listening) Do you have Farante? It sounds like he is an awful character. OK." I hang up the call.

"He says Farante is gone, out of the country, little Henderson too."

Julie takes my hand, "Let's get out of here. We need a break. Do you think Joe wants to go back to school?"

We walk outside.

"I am headed home; I have a new job to start soon. I think I also have some money to look for." Forester sticks out his hand.

"You do know everyone will deny it right?" Phillip states.

"Yup, until Jamaica finds it for us, I will call you next week." Forester looks at Caruso, "You need a lift?"

Caruso looks at me, "Yeah, I have no car."

"Give my sister a hug when you see her."

"I will."

"Dad, I think I am going back to my dorm. I have classes Monday."

"You ready for that?"

"I am, plus with the keystone cops inside I think I will be OK."

"I guess I got to let you go."

"This case was better than the last one. You didn't shoot anyone!"

Joe walks away and I have a pit in my stomach. Julie looks at me, "Since Henderson's office is close by, I will ask that they keep an eye on him every once in a while."

Phillip is standing by the car. "Let's go."

"What else did Jilly say?"

"He said he wired me a large fee since he had access to some money. He also said the guy in the car today wasn't going to kill us, just a scare tactic."

"That is a real shame," Phillip says.

"He also said we should call him if we are going to look for the football money, it seems he persuaded Farante to put it back but he would not say where it is."

Julie starts walking towards the car pulling me along, "That Jilly is some character."

"I need to ask him something."

I dial Jilly. I listen for a second, laugh, and put the phone on speaker, 'I AM SORRY BUT THE NUMBER YOU ARE TRYING TO REACH IS NO LONGER IN SERVICE.

Epilogue:

"OK, I get it, the last case made no sense. I needed the last few months to try and sort things out. To be honest, I am not sure I can do that. We did not solve anything. This case had multiple levels of potential bad guys, which turned out to be supposedly on the good side, but I am not so sure. There is still the college football fund that is either missing or never existed. I am sure it exists because every few years some expose article comes out and a low-level executive from a shoe company goes to jail or some coach is forced to resign from his lofty position in the world as a football coach. This coach inevitably resurfaces at another school – like there is no one else qualified. I guess you have to admire the loyalty of these so-called boosters being devoted to their colleges. Then we had the billion-dollar CIA fund that has been in existence for years. All those government agents, the Lees, Johnson, small Henderson and how can we forget Jilly and Farante, I am not sure what was accomplished. They were all chasing the money and each other. We got paid by the FBI, at least some of our expenses, we got paid by the NFL to look for the slush fund which never appeared or maybe disappeared or was stolen by one or more of the knuckleheads, but we hit the jackpot when

Jilly was true to his word and wired to me our fee. I have no idea how he wired me the money, but then again, I guess he can get that type of information if anyone can. I transferred the money immediately to another account. I have no idea why I think that would hide it.

Joe went back to class to finish the semester; He seems to be enjoying it. He heads down here when he can to enjoy some time on the water. Caruso and Sarah are still doing the commute back and forth from New York to Florida. We have gotten together a few times for dinner, he even pays. Phillip has been sequestered in his hotel for the last six weeks finishing a book he promised his agent. He says I need to keep an open mind when I read the proofs. Forester has set up shop in the NFL's office down here. He is traveling a lot. I give him six months.

Since we have no case on the horizon it feels rather good to have the days to myself. Thank you, Jilly, for being very generous in paying our fee. I probably should not mention this again since we do not know exactly where the money came from. I asked Julie to move into the house with me which I think was a moot point, but I needed to ask. She said yes which I think we both took for granted since she had no place to live down here. She commutes about thirty miles to the FBI office in Miami. Her days are busy with various investigations and of course, loads of paperwork. That is the benefit of working with me, absolutely no paperwork, ever."

CHAPTER .5

A NEW YORK STATE OF MIND

Julie has just left for work and I am padding around the house until the rain is supposed to stop which according to the TV should be by noon. We rented this house before we left New York but the area and the house are perfect. It's a semi-gated area, a guardhouse without gates. We have walking trails, tennis and basketball courts, and a clubhouse. This size house is perfect, 3 bedrooms all on one floor is ideal. All these houses were built within the last 5 years so everything has that new look. The community handles all the outside maintenance. I am on a waiting list to buy a house here which the leasing agent says should be within four months. That should give us time to decide if everything down here is right for us. Even the furniture that came with the house works and best of all you can rent a boat which of course I did. With everyone down here, it's hard to think we would ever go back to New York.

I stare out at the gray churning water in the canal and the boats bouncing up and down in the rough surf. On days like this, I get bored easily. My phone is ringing from the kitchen counter. Hopefully, Joe calling to say he will be down this weekend.

"Hello?? (listening) How are you, John? (listening) I am sorry to hear that. I tried to get in touch with him over the last month to say hello. I know he comes down here to get away from the New York winters and I wanted to get together for coffee when he did come. Gino will be missed. I liked him. (Listening) Thank you, that's nice of you to say. (Listening) A safe deposit box that he wanted me to have? John, I know you are his son and my lawyer but is this a good idea? (Listening) OK, I will come up."

I have a bad feeling about this.

Jamaica Biltmore: Interference

Book II

Tom Greco